Thread Of Life

Thread Of Life

Written by
Frances R. Kubitz

Illustrated by
Frederick T. Kubitz

ISBN 0-9670086-0-3
Copyright © 1999 by Frances R. Kubitz
Jacket Cover Illustration Copyright © by Frederick T. Kubitz
Printed in the United States of America 1999

ACKNOWLEDGMENTS

These pages are filled with names of and references to a cadre that hovers. I give my heartfelt thanks to them through my voice in this book, and by prayers into perpetuity.

Medical detail and encouragement to do the story came from Dr. Saint George Tucker Aufranc. The editing and comments such as, 'Let me congratulate you on a memorable, intriguing, and passionate story', were put forth by my editor, Maria E. denBoer.

The painting, the creation of Fritz Kubitz, on the dust jacket is an area in Maine called the **Thread of Life**. I expect no less of him.

The polio experiences are taken from fact although the story line is a work of fiction. Some character names, locations, and times have been changed.

TABLE OF CONTENTS

THAT WHICH IS BELIEVED IS LOVE

PROLOGUE

State in Grip of Pandemic!

Headlines in the *Chicago Tribune* scream "POLIO" in four-inch black letters.

It is summer, and the death count mounts throughout the state. Health Departments scramble to meet the needs of every hospital. The governor of Illinois, Dwight H. Green, enlists volunteers from the military to aid in the emergency. Funds from the National Foundation for Infantile Paralysis pour into the state.

Evil-looking machines called iron lungs are installed in makeshift isolation wards.

Every effort is expended to alert the public through the media about the dangers of contagion. Despite the horror stories circulating and the warnings to keep out of crowds, the Chicago Railroad Fair, county fairs, youth camps, carnivals, swimming pools, and theaters continue to flourish.

Some worried parents keep their children at home the entire summer, but despite their caution, many became ill. No one knows exactly how the disease is transmitted.

Poliomyelitis, after a few dormant years, and smoldering in small outbreaks, has risen forcibly to prey on children. In the virulent outbreak this year, young adults are also stricken. Hundreds become unwilling victims. They come from remote farms, rural towns, and crowded cities. The greedy disease tramples hopes and dreams, and shatters young lives. Gone in a twisted moment are youth and ability.

Long strings of statistics begin to pile up as mothers' tears spill in hospital corridors across the state. The cries of grieving relatives can be heard across telephone lines and in churches.

Outside many hospitals, a merciless sun beats down on wickedly gleaming iron lungs as they are, one by one, carefully rolled off ramps from waiting trucks. Deliverymen never think about the gruesomeness of this, for it's all in a day's work. They, like most people, are relieved the machines aren't for them. The business of a healthy ongoing life absorbs most people.

Across the country numerous states are beginning to report cases, and by the end of the summer forty thousand will be recorded.

From the *New York Times: In Upstate New York seventy-two new cases and two more deaths were reported to the State Health Department. The upstate case total since January rose to 957. There have been twentysix deaths. New York City officials warned that the epidemic was only half over, the city had 1,773 cases.*

National health officials are filled with terror over the runaway epidemic, for the disease has no cure.

Other countries with epidemic outbreaks are also in the news. Czechoslovakia has nine thousand cases. Prague is building the largest hospital in the world for the treatment of poliomyelitis. Sister Elizabeth Kenny, originator of methods for treating polio, tours five European countries presenting scientific evidence of her successful treatments.

In far-off Hudson Bay, a doctor in Chesterfield Inlet radios an appeal for help and places under quarantine a vast area straddling forty thousand miles of treeless barrens. A Royal Canadian plane brings in five topnotch medical men with three hundred pounds of diagnostic and physiotherapeutic equipment from Winnipeg. They find the stricken Eskimos talking of bad magic, hate spells, and the need for tribal ceremonies to banish evil spirits. The medical team diagnoses sixty people with polio, and a few of whom will have to be air-lifted to Winnipeg. Thirteen have already died.

The Royal Canadian Mounted Police have some difficulty enforcing the quarantine because the Eskimos are nomadic. They travel by dog teams seeking seal, caribou, and furs. The temperature in winter averages 32 degrees below zero, but even that temperature does not keep out polio. To maintain and localize the epidemic, measures are intensified.

Although a lot of effort is expended globally, sometimes little results are seen. The ravages of such a feared disease mounts.

Chapter 1

❧

ONSET

In late May restless dark clouds move into Champaign, Illinois, bringing a prowling killer. On the outskirts of town an emergency isolation hospital is set up in a vacant building, as health authorities expect a surge of polio patients throughout the summer. The arrangements for the hospital and staff are overseen by Dr. Max Arzberg, a pediatric neurologist from the local hospital.

Francy Holland, a journalism student attending the University of Illinois, never believes in her wildest dreams she will ever come remotely near the doctor or these preparations. Paul Davidson, who dates her, never gives any of the preparations a second thought and—

Friday, August 28, 11:00 a.m.,
Administration Building, University of Illinois

—here we go. As I contemplated the questionnaire on the desk in front of me, I was caught off-guard by the fact that my eyes were one place and my mind another. What was distracting me was how I was feeling, but I couldn't quite put my finger on what was wrong.

Oddly, the sun outside seemed more pronounced, and conversations stood out. My self-awareness was also heightened, and appeared to crawl relentlessly toward something vaguely impending. I had a strange need to pull things in close to remember, and my present impressions etched as though they might be the last. In a chilling way they were.

I shook off the intrusion with annoyance, finished the answer to the last question on the student form, and returned my pen to my purse. Handing my fall schedule in to an attendant at the office, I swiftly leave the administration building and head for the cafeteria to meet Paul Davidson for our lunch date.

Paul, a junior majoring in Architecture, has lived in Champaign all his life and had attended high school with me. We didn't begin dating until we were both in college, and during the first year found we were in love steering toward a lasting relationship. I wear his fraternity pin, which signifies we are an item.

As I crossed the quadrangle, I felt some relief that I had finished selecting sophomore courses for the fall. But with the relief I also felt strangely ill. It wasn't exactly summer flu, but something else. I had been bothered by nagging head-aches and a mild, stiff neck for several days. Oddly, the skin on my back and legs hurt in tiny pinpricks.

When I arrived at the cafeteria in the Union building, I saw Paul waiting for me at a small table covered with papers. His tall frame was bent over the sketches, and his jeans and shirt were spattered with paint.

"You must have come from art class," I said as I slid into a chair across from him, giving him a smile.

Paul grinned back as he rose, and then his expression quickly changed to one of concern. "Are you all right? You look a little under the weather. Do you really want lunch?"

"I'd love a fruit salad," I said wearily, "and some water to take aspirin for this headache I can't shake."

I didn't tell him more, but knew he would later persist and ask probing questions.

When Paul returned with our order, I asked about the drawings.

"These something new?"

Paul nodded, then showed me the ideas for a design con-test he was entering sponsored by the *Chicago Tribune*. We decided he had a good chance of winning.

As I studied the sketches, my mind took another circuit. He is much too handsome, his hands belong to a pianist, and his intensity when he looks at me makes me quiver inside. Paul has appeal, and it cames from his stature, his intelle-gence, and his single minded concern for me. I am always proud to be in his company.

Paul and I are "townies," who live at home instead of on campus. Our houses are six blocks apart in the western por-tion of Champaign, and we like to take long walks to the downtown area, have picnics in the country on our bicycles, or drive to state parks out of town.

When we finished our brief lunch, Paul gathered his drawings and we walked slowly to his car while he queried me about my fall schedule and how I was really feeling.

"Your class load sounds a little heavy, and you're going to be running all over the campus. Maybe by mid-term you may want to change a course. But I don't like the sound of your symptons, and I think you should check in with your doctor," he said, giving my arm a pinch. "You could be coming down with something, and just before classes are to start."

"I know, I don't relish beginning a full schedule feeling as I do. It will probably just go away in a day or so."

We arrived at his car and once inside he gathered me to him in an embrace I sorely needed. I had quickened heart-beats as we exchanged breathless kisses as his hands caressed my back taking nerve endings to their limits. He put so much commitment into his kisses it made my head swim, and I felt a profound sadness when we drew apart.

Arriving at my house, I readied to get out of the car, and Paul turned toward me, his voice low and insistent, "Don't forget to call the doctor for an appointment, Francy, don't delay. I don't want you to take any chances."

I promised I would call as I remembered our family doctor kept Saturday hours. When I got inside the house, I quickly gave Dr. Collins a call, and was scheduled to see him at 11:30 the following morning. I explained to my parents I thought I was running a slight fever.

Saturday, (Downtown Champaign, in the Federal Bank Building, Second Floor.)

I walked into Dr. Collins' office and was immediately greeted by him.

He studied me with shrewd eyes behind silver-rimmed glasses, and directed me to a leather armchair for some general conversation. When we were seated opposite each other he asked the reasons for my visit.

He was aware that mild tremors were cruising my body making me shake. I could not stop the tremors, and felt embarrassed by this new, unwanted affliction. I discussed the headaches, and the leg and thigh pain.

Dr. Collins spoke softly. "First, I need to check your general health. I'll see if you have a temperature, check your blood pressure, and test your reflexes."

He took my arm when we went to his examining room as though I had suddenly become feeble. He helped me onto the padded table, and there, among several observations, found I had an elevated temperature, poor reflexes in both knees, and both eyes very sensitive to light. He spent some time having me describe the pain in my legs and showing him where they hurt.

We returned to the office chairs, and he pulled his chair so close our knees almost touched. He looked directly into my eyes, and began an explanation of meningitis and similar diseases.

"Back up a minute, Dr. Collins," I interrupted, "you're not meaning me?"

Several times he tried to allay my anxiety, but I was starting to prepare myself for the worst. I couldn't put off the realization any longer. Then it came: I had to have a spinal tap.

Fear leaped into my heart and showed in my eyes. Dr. Collins became more somber, looked down at the floor with a tense expression, and I sensed I was breaking his heart. He had known me since I was five, and he now knew things he couldn't tell me.

"I will make an appointment for you at the isolation hospital," he continued, "for this afternoon. There you will have the spinal tap performed. It isn't painful, and they will know in a short while what is going on with you. The chief of staff out there is an excellent doctor. I will speak with him, tell him all about you. I don't think this is really polio you have, but we must be on the safe side."

He said all this while holding my hands and gently emphasizing his words with pressure.

Oh no. Not this afternoon, not so soon, I complained to myself wanting to cry, but not in front of Dr. Collins.

Quivering with new fear as I prepared to leave the office, I looked at him, waiting for him to recant and make it all right, but his eyes conveyed a message that I sadly had to acknowledge.

I walked home on a beautiful, warm day, seeing my reflection in store windows as I passed. I guessed this would be the last time I would be able to stroll, skip, or run. With a suppressed sob, I quickly did all of them no matter who was watching.

This is my life, I told the figure in the windows, my time to capture. I have to remember what these feelings are like, the motions, and the freedom.

I didn't know where those ideas came from, but they were urgent, and I took great pleasure in my exertions. I was also aware something insidious was beginning to strangle my life.

The image of the slim, skipping woman left behind in the store windows moved on. She wore shoulder-length, warm brown hair in soft curls, and had recently applied pink lipstick. Her bright smile and gray-blue eyes didn't show her inner turmoil, or that she normally had a positive outlook on life.

The windows didn't reflect the fact that swimming, cycling, and ice skating were her favorite sports, nor did they shimmer with her hopes of becoming a journalist.

The large panes of glass were also lacking the facts that her views of the world were naive, sometimes mystical, but most times, imaginative. And, as the fleeting images quietly faded, so did that of the young woman.

Nearing home, I wondered if my personality would also cancel out, and if I would become someone I don't know or like. I chided myself with that thought as I ran up the front steps of our house thinking maybe by some stroke of luck I'd be let off the hook.

Dr. Collins in the meantime, unbeknounst to me, phoned my mother to alert her to what he had found. He also explained the ramifications of polio.

My mother looked composed when I entered the living room, but I sensed she wasn't. She suggested that I lie down for a while, and I welcomed the suggestion. A half hour later the phone rang, and my mother came to my room to tell me that a nurse from the isolation hospital had called to instruct that I not bring any personal belongings with me as they would provide the necessities. Also not to wear any jewelry, but old clothes and shoes that could be burned. My mother and I exchanged glances that told of our dread.

In my bedroom, I walked about, touching and memorizing cherished belongings, then played favorite music records while rummaging in the closet for the clothes. I found a cotton skirt, a blouse that had seen better days, and a pair of scuffed sandals. It was hard to believe I would never see these articles of clothing again.

I put the temporary outfit on, feeling like a criminal on the way to jail. The guilt had started. Slowly I removed from my finger a small gold friendship ring Paul had given me, and placed it inside my jewelry box next to his fraternity pin.

Fine goose bumps traveled my arms as I defiantly thought: I will wear these again when I return home.

Paul and I wanted to see the world, conquer art, start fresh with new ideas, and forge a life that seemed to be meant for us to be together. We looked no further beyond each other. Now what was going to happen to those plans? Would he find someone else?

Chapter 2

❦

ONE HUNDRED AND ONE

My father's car pulled up in the driveway, and I saw time had eaten up the minutes, for the moment to go had come. Dark visions swam in my head as a strangled cry of despair tried to reach my throat. Quickly banking it down, I again had to remind myself that all this might well be a false alarm.

Brave thoughts for one who knows little of what lay ahead.

Before leaving the house I took time to pet and hug our family cat, Betty, and wondered if I'd ever see her again. I also wondered how Paul will take the news. Somehow, everything had become very dramatic in a very short time.

The trip out to the countryside was much too short, and my tension mounted with each driven mile. I felt it in myself, and I felt it in my parents. We arrived in the visitors' parking lot of the hospital all too soon, and the place didn't look as threatening as I had expected. However, large signs on the double front doors that read, "Hospital in Quarantine," "No Admittance—Only Medical Personnel With Patients," and "Absolutely No Smoking," warned this was serious.

Being expected, we were met at the doors by Lynn Goddard, a nurse holding papers my parents had to sign. They were also instructed to wait outside on the steps, as a doctor would see them soon. Then my father signed the documents to release me to the care of this facility.

Gradually Lynn ushered me in from the sunshine, and I don't remember if anyone of us said anything. I entered without any possessions except for the clothes on my back. A sensation of extreme fear swept over me, and I hung back as I looked through the outside doors in a last futile appeal.

My destiny can't be here? !

I reluctantly gave up the last shred of control over my life and committed myself to go through whatever was ahead, and felt very alone.

Gritting my teeth without realizing it, I finally released them when Lynn fastened a name tag to my wrist and asked how I was feeling. I said I was apprehensive. Lynn's kind words softened the moment, but I sensed that nothing from that moment on was going to be easy. There was nothing in my mind to steel against the inevitable, no outside help, and now, no escape.

Looking around, I saw this was a different type of hospital. First, it was immaculate. Then, the sounds were strange, and there was no evidence of smiles, flowers, posters, or music. The light in the hallway was so bright it hurt my eyes, and it bounced off pale green walls to shiny tile floors. Supply boxes were stacked along one wall, shiny oxygen tanks stood in rows, and a pervading smell of disinfectant clung to everything.

Here, the personnel moved briskly on soft rubber soles, and strange wheezing sounds filled the air.

It took exactly twenty hesitant footsteps for me to reach an overcrowded small room, where I was given a short cotton open-backed gown to wear. Once dressed, I surrendered my clothes to never see again. I was helped up by Lynn onto a white padded operating table, and sat there swinging my legs. Immediately two doctors came into the room and introduced themselves as Dr. Arzberg and Dr. Morris. I noticed the men were handsome, young, and friendly.

Dr. Arzberg picked up my wrist and read my name tag. "Are you a student at the university?"

"Yes," I answered lightly, "a sophomore, and my friends call me Francy."

"Age, Francy?" He asked as he moved around to inspect my back.

"Nineteen," I replied, hoping to delay all this.

The two doctors exchanged a quick look.

Dr. Arzberg, with gentle hands helped me lie down, and turned me onto my right side on the narrow table for the spinal tap.

Bless him, Dr. Collins was right, I never felt what was being done. The smell of alcohol that drifted about the room however, was a constant reminder of where I was.

Dr. Arzberg then explained the spinal tap procedure. "I will prepare a small area on your lower back by swabbing it with antiseptic."

I liked the sound of his voice.

"Then I will give you a local anesthetic before doing the lumbar puncture."

Dr. Arzberg took a small 3cc syringe holding 1% xylocaine with a 25-gauge needle from a nearby tray.

I already hated this, but decided now was not the time to argue. Several microscopes sitting nearby on a counter caught my attention. Dr. Morris explained that he would study under a microscope slides holding my spinal fluid. The slides would quickly detail the white cell count, and also the type of disease present. Asking many questions in my nervousness, I was politely and truthfully answered.

"All right," Dr. Arzberg said, "I'll explain everything I'm doing. There will be a pinch and we'll be done."

He turned to the same tray with efficiency and picked up a 10cc syringe with a long 25-gauge needle. He saw that I had twisted around to see what he was doing, and as he held the needle aloft he tried to reassure me.

"It doesn't matter the size, the results are the same. I ask that you remain very still. Just a small nip, and then we'll be through."

He inserted the needle below the third lumbar vertebra into the spinal canal. Withdrawing a small amount of spinal fluid, he then passes the syringe to Dr. Morris.

"That's all there is to it. Please rest, Francy, for a while longer."

Dr. Arzberg patted my shoulder, then placed a warm white blanket over me.

Both doctors went over to the microscopes to examine the spinal fluid for cell count and differential. Their voices were low, and I couldn't hear anything they were saying. (I learned later what they saw.)

They were looking for white cells/red cells and their

numerical distribution. What they saw was an over-abundance of white cells, indicating a viral infection. The number of cells was over a thousand per cc, which showed that the degree of infection was severe.

All the time the doctors worked, I could see my parents through a small window, quietly talking. Fifteen minutes later I saw their faces as Dr. Arzberg informed them of my condition. My father shook his head in denial, my mother dropped her head, and covered her mouth with her hand. Dr. Arzberg moved closer to her and pressed her hands in his, talking earnestly and telling her he would do all he could.

They had been told their daughter had the highest white cell count the doctors had seen so far, and that she had acute anterior polio.

This, I was not told.

When Doctor Arzberg came back into the room, he took some time to explain the hospital routine. He also said I would have to stay for a quarantine period of two weeks. That's the only part I really heard.

The doctors, each taking an arm, helped me down from the table, and over to a nearby wheelchair. I asked for permission to walk to my room. Dr. Arzberg, with his first smile of the day, gave me permission.

Wearing a new robe and my old sandals, with Lynn holding my arm in assistance, I took cautious steps down the corridor. I was wobbly, still had those annoying shakes, and now my ears were ringing.

Dr. Arzberg stood in the doorway to the lab, watching thinking about his latest patient.

'Lord, so young, with so much in front of her. What this disease will do, we both don't yet know.'

I passed two large wards filled with cribs. In the cribs were babies and children of all ages, moaning, crying, and pleading for their mommies. Lynn told me, compassion in her voice, "Nurses and aides in these wards do backbreaking work on each six-hour shift. Each day the children have to be bathed and their positions shifted often to protect against bedsores. The pediatric staff is in charge of diapers, IVs, medication, clean bedding, and food for those who can eat. Despite the grueling schedules, they somehow have time for the soothing of tears, reassurance of fear, and the introduction of a new toy."

Reality started to sink in as I was introduced to the pain, heartache, and despair of others. I, too, was now an inmate in a prison that housed tragic circumstances. It was no longer 'them and those,' it was now 'we and us.'

The noises increased as we approached the iron lung ward. These I had read about, but had no idea how awful they sounded, and how big they were. One room held seven iron lung machines, all occupied. Three empty ones lay in wait in the outside corridor. Shock and curiosity halted me as I became swamped with emotion. I realized these machines were for breathing, and these adults and children couldn't breathe.

Interest overcame my fear, and I walked into the ward and moved closer to a large, shiny cylinder in a creamy-yellow color. It encased the patient with bulbar polio, one of the deadly forms of the disease. The respirator was five feet long and was placed horizontally on supporting racks. It could be moved on wheels and encircled the patient from neck to feet. The head rested outside the tank on a pillowed platform with the neck gripped by a sponge rubber gasket. The gasket kept the air pressure inside the iron lung from escaping. Windows or portals that could be opened, were located on each side of the cylinders so nurses could bathe, medicate, and assist the patients.

Great compressing bellows beneath the tanks kept the precious air moving. They expanded and contracted with a ceaseless rhythm. Air pressure forced the patients to inhale and exhale because their respiratory systems had shut down due to paralysis. The patient could only talk during the short spell of exhalation. Breathing rate, amount of oxygen, heart rate, and bodily functions were monitored by gauges, dials, bags, and other machines. Patients inside the iron lungs could not eat or swallow solid food, thus they were fed nourishing liquids through a feeding tube. Because they had only facial and vocal movements left, they had literally become a part of the machinery.

The relentless activity of the bellows going up and down, and the sound of the wheezing noises they made were loud and frightening. Trained attendants on rotation every four hours watched each iron lung. I looked into the mirror in front of one patient's face, and was startled when the man reflected there winked at me. I gave him a brave smile. Although I smiled, I saw that this was a terrible way to live. No jokes here. Terror was alive and rampant.

Chapter 3

❦

REALITY CHECK

My private room, all of twelve feet square, awaited. I noticed it had a small twin-size bed, bedside table, metal floor lamp, and outside screened window. The room was newly painted in pale green, and had an off-white linoleum floor. An intravenous stand with filled bottles of clear liquid sat ominously in a corner. My room also had a fixed glassed-in window near the hall so I could be observed.

I'm not sure I like that.

I had drawn quiet stares the time I had been on the way to my room. I now realized I was the only patient in the hospital who could walk.

Dr. Arzberg also had taken particular interest in my journey down the corridor, for Lynn said he had watched the entire trip.

I wanted the bed moved next to the outside window, and it was done immediately. This position would be temporary. The room's floor, bed, lamp and equipment had been recently wiped down with disinfectant, and smelled strongly of it. This would be done often, I was told, because I had a contagious infection that could be transmitted.

Although I know this, I refused to give it a name.

Feeling somewhat dizzy, with my headache starting to reach outer limits, I loathed placing myself in that bed; it seemed like total surrender. Since there wasn't anything else to do, I took off the robe and sandals, and slid in. The sheets were cold and unfriendly.

A few minutes later my parents arrived at the screened window. This was the only place where I could receive visitors. My parents, and Paul, with special permission, were the only ones allowed. My parents asked who I wanted called, and if I would like them to bring anything back. I asked them to phone Paul.

They looked devastated as they left for home.

Then I was given a small cup of apple juice and a small white pill to swallow, and was instructed to lay flat without a pillow. Soon hypodermic needles, pills, IVs, and liquids became the routine. I drifted in and out of disturbed random sleep all afternoon.

I awoke to see my white radio next to my bed as well as a comb and brush, lipstick, and some coins for the soft drink machine.

Already there were messages and two telegrams to read. I was having difficulty moving my arms and legs, and just wanted to be left alone. Also, the sense of time and orientation had become lost.

I thought all this was going to be temporary.

At home, my mother frantically calls friends and relatives to find out what she can about polio and its treatment, and what can be done for me. She also phones Paul to confirm that what he had thought was only a mild illness, was much more.

My parents think this is the last they will hear from Paul, but he surprises everyone, especially himself.

Hours later an aide came into the room to read the messages of love and hope from friends and relatives, and tuned my radio to station WILL. I listened to the university station play classical music until the late bulletins were read. Wonder of wonders, I heard my own name and age being reported.

"Miss Frances Holland of Champaign, nineteen years old, was admitted to the isolation hospital at two o'clock this afternoon. She is the one hundred and first patient to be registered in Champaign County with polio this summer."

I felt a curious dissociation from the news as a different type of struggle was demanding all my resources. As the sun went down on my first day in purgatory, I, too, descended into that bottomless pit.

Forty-eight hours dragged by in wavering blackness. Where I had gone I didn't know, but I had seen images I would never have imagined. Sometime during those silent hours an essence had slipped away, and I had felt a strong need to pray.

In the prayers I asked God to take care of everyone including our cat. When I finished, tired from the long list, I felt warmed by a light that seems to advance from the corner of my room to my bedside. Then my right hand was touched. I became infused with brilliant light, and I felt love.

Although no one was there, I heard the words, "I Am Here."

I tried to answer but felt strong resistance. Slowly I left my body in the bed as though it was the most natural thing in the world to do, and soared to meet vague people who seemed to know me. Five distinct shapes moved toward me, and each had something to say. A feeling of great love made itself known, but I sensed that I had to go back somewhere and could not join them.

I became confused as I was told I had a tough fight ahead, but I would make it, and they would be behind me in support. Lastly, they said there were important unfulfilled things left for me to do.

Although I was reluctant to leave their protective and illusive embrace, I mentally consented to go back. A peace of gigantic proportions filled my mind. During all this time I never opened my eyes.

Dr. Arzberg, as was his custom, also prayed. "Francy Holland's life hangs by a thread, Dear Lord. Keep your hand on her."

I gradually awoke from a coma and knew I had been transformed. Awareness brought wracking pain throughout my body. The pain crescendoed over and over, like an unrelenting machine I couldn't stop. I couldn't locate the source of the pain, but felt like I had been stung by hundreds of bees. I ground my teeth and moaned in my suffering, as I tried to retreat to the dark.

My mind was going through a torment of conflict. I was in anguish at being sick, guilty for giving so many people grief over my suffering, and angry that my world had been invaded by so many strangers.

When I first opened my eyes, Dr. Max Arzberg swam into my vision, fuzzy at first, then more clearly.

"There you are." He said, pleased about something. "You sure blew my statistics all to hell, young lady."

He continued to tap the clipboard he held with pages telling my story. A secret person resided on those pages, one I couldn't see. But I could clearly see this man in charge of me. His crisp white jacket fit a tall lean physique, he was nice-looking with even features, and had a take-charge attitude. He had dark brown hair that fell over his forehead on one side, and compassionate, deep blue eyes.

"Now that you are awake," he continued shuffling his feet, "we will soon be seeing and testing what this disease is doing."

I asked many questions, but didn't like the answers. The doctor was very direct, and his tone of voice was low and calming.

"Frankly, you were not expected to make it, and the iron-lung positioned outside this room is in case your breathing becomes more difficult."

I looked at the machine outside the observation window and decided I'd rather be reduced to ashes than be placed in it. I didn't want to become one of 'them.'

Blandly I told the doctor, "I'd rather you shoot me instead." Although his eyes flickered a moment, like a lit candle in a faint breeze, he resumed a benign expression. He seemed unconcerned about my bold request.

Dr. Arzberg saw that I was trying to digest all that he was telling me while silent tears started to spill into my hair. I couldn't brush them away, for I couldn't move my arms. I found I couldn't move my legs either. This is how a nightmare becomes real.

While the doctor quickly dabbed at my tears with a tissue, I looked up at him in anguish. He consoled me again with the tone of his voice, shushing my fears.

"You are doing fine, Francy. You have passed a crisis. I

have been with you throughout it. First, let's confront your breathing and then the headache. I want you to cough for me now, and let me know if you feel places I touch."

He moved to the end of my bed and lifted the covers.

I struggled to comply to his questions. Some sort of lead weight was also sitting on my chest. He touched my feet, then worked up my legs.

Can I feel his touch? No.

He gently lifted both my arms and moved my shoulders asking me each time if I could hold them up. His expression was very serious and intent. Then he asked me to count to ten in one breath.

I thought in annoyance I could do that, but found I couldn't. I tried again, but he shook his head for me to stop. He demonstrated to a nurse standing by, the technique to help me breathe. Positioning my hands over my heart, he gently pressed down, doing so several times evenly spaced in time. He explained to her that she had to be gentle or she would bruise the ribs.

After about five pushes he said, "That's enough for now. Repeat this again about once every hour. She will normally try to help and increase the strength."

Then he nodded to a waiting nurse, stepped aside and a quick hypo was directed to my right hip. As I started to fade, leaving questions behind, I welcomed the trip.

I'm not ready for this paralysis stuff.

A pleasant female voice intruded, "Ah, ah, don't go away. We're about to give you a bath."

My eyes stared out of a pale face and I struggled to speak.

Another nearby voice said, "Wait until the exhalation, but don't hurry, you'll get the hang of it."

Panic and feelings of hysteria rose like a cloud in my chest.

How many breaths did I have? And would there be enough? How do I stay out of that iron lung?

Softly cool hands encased my face and I shifted my eyes

to the right. Dr. Arzberg gave me a tentative smile. "We are pleased to see you can breathe on your own, Francy. You are making progress now. After your bath and a few more tests, we will see if you can breathe a little better. In the meantime, use your mind to relax; there is nothing to fear here. We are with you every second."

I did as he instructed and saw him nod with approval. Then he disappeared from my range of vision.

Falling asleep again, I awoke as my own bath was in progress. I had some sensation of movement, but could not help out. I could only move my eyes, hear, breathe, and smell the soap. That was all. Feeling awful mentally, physically, and emotionally, I wanted to give up, I wanted out of this.

There was no one here who would let me.

Besides, I needed to go to the bathroom, and there wasn't one nearby. It hadn't yet occurred to me that I couldn't get to one on my own anyway.

Then I touched on abject anger and hate in my mind. I was startled by its ugliness. All that writhing in the dark side didn't suit me, but I stayed there to get a better look.

If this is the devil's work, I know what it looks like for the first time, and I'm not sure I want to be one of its converts. Yet, if I let go, and can really have control over living or dying, which way will I roll?

Dr. Arzberg's voice barged into my private musing. "Think you'd like to help me?" He had seen the grim set of my mouth, and guessed I was dealing with mental images that were not too pleasant.

Suddenly I was moving, got dizzy, and realized my bed was being shifted near the outside window. When I looked left, I saw the concern on the faces of Paul and my parents. They stood outside the window looking in and wanting to tell me many things, but I wanted to shrivel into an invisible ball.

I heard all their news, and was mildly interested in what

friends and relatives were saying. I actually had trouble concentrating, and lashed my head back and forth on the pillow,
for it was the only thing I could do.

Then I asked on a halting exhale, "They say I am better.
How?"

I looked at Paul for confirmation, and he came close to
the screen to say, "Dr. Arzberg has a surprise for you after we
leave. I miss you, our talks, and everything. My school schedule is pretty tough this year. I have to take calculus and will
need some help. Stan can see me through. Otherwise, all the
art and architectural courses are my speed. Get better
Francy, and I'll see you tomorrow."

He smiled and my heart ached.

I took it all in, in an abstract way, wondering what I felt
about him and if it would do any good.

My parents chatted with me for ten minutes, and I was
rolled back to my former position in the middle of the room.
I saw the day outside was still mockingly sunny and cheerfully warm. The knowledge was an awful hurt. I was
practically choking with rage.

Dr. Arzberg stood by the door to the room not wanting to
intrude.

Later he sat on a little fold-up chair and concentrated on
his mission for being in the hospital chapel.

"Lord, keep your hand on my patients and staff. Guide
me in decisions, help me to help them. I apologize for sin-
gling out one patient. However, you know who she is. Every
breath I take I freely give to her to save her. Please intervene
for me. Give her hope and the will to survive."

When Max came out of the chapel, he felt further drained.
It had been a long spell, and he didn't feel like resting, though
he needed to. He knew he had to have a clear mind and lots
of energy, for too many unknowns were swirling about, and
he had to be on call for all of them.

Chapter 4

❦

PAINFUL LESSONS

More merciless time elapsed before next I opened my eyes again. It was night, the same day. There were two smiling nurses in the room, and Dr. Arzberg was standing at the foot of the bed writing on my chart. I saw a small metal machine near my bed that resembled a steaming pressure cooker. One of the waiting nurses moved toward me, and took off the resting sheet.

To my horror, I realized I was hooked up to several lines including a catheter.

So, that's how they take care of my needs, since I can't walk to the bathroom.

The nurse applied a pale salve over my entire body from neck to toe, explaining what had been done for me in the past several hours.

During all this, I am nude. More humiliation. Too late for embarrassment, so I learned instant detachment. Hey, I've been out of my body, I can do this. Maybe I can also become invisible if I put my mind to it.

Next, the nurse opened the machine at the top, and extracted with tongs a roll of misting grey wool. She neatly wound the strip around my right leg. Then she did the left. Roll after roll was wound around my arms and torso until I was completely covered. Sixteen rolls were applied, and she was most careful about not disturbing the thin tubes running from my body.

To my surprise the soothing and penetrating heat were heavenly. And best of all, it took away the pain, which erased the depression.

And thank God, I'm entirely covered!

Dr. Arzberg looked over my wool strips, adjusted my legs in a more comfortable position, and asked if I would like some cold ginger ale. My eyes lit up, and I nodded. He brought some back in with a bent straw, and held my head up a little so I could sip.

I was told they would repeat the "Sister Kenny" treatment around-the-clock each time the wool became cool until

I no longer needed it. I didn't ask how long that would be.

It turned out to be three weeks.

Before Dr. Arzberg left my room, he leaned over to get my complete attention. He told me something I would never forget. "Do not waste precious energy on anger, Francy. Use it to get better."

I had been denying everything that was around me, and most things that were happening. My eyes squeezed shut.

Don't I still have control over my own body? Is the control all gone, and am I left a prisoner in this shell? If this is it, what can I do to end it? My cheek was softly patted, and my eyes flew open.

Dr. Arzberg, assessing my condition, said, "All things being equal, which they are not, I caution you to take stock of what you have. Try to accept the reality of your loss, Francy. Work through the grief. You need to concentrate on more positive thoughts."

Is he now reading my mind?

I digested his words. His penetrating steady gaze held mine. We made a firm and lasting connection at that moment. I felt some of my ideas tilt, and I struggled to right them. He felt his professional demeanor start to slip. Did he dare to cross the line? His heart would decide.

Lynn became my steady nurse each day and I was able to ask her a lot of questions. She explained that the wool strips used as my pain aid had been cut from Army blankets. She also said that military personnel had been enlisted as volunteers to work in the polio wards all across the country.

Since the epidemic was at its worst in Illinois, I soon got used to being fed and bathed by men, all soldiers. They were each very kind, sympathetic, and neutral in these very personal duties.

Hours later, I snuggled in my strange wool cocoon getting the blessed relief so desperately needed. My ease, however, would soon be disturbed.

Dr. Arzberg came in and sat in a chair by my side as a

nurse replaced cooled wool strips with hot ones. "Francy, I'll not pull my punches; you need to be told. You are in a state of paralysis from your neck to your toes. You breathe on your own, but now a new crisis has to be faced."

I asked, "How long will I remain this way?"

"That's the crisis. I'm not sure, it depends on a few factors and your state of mind."

His sapphire eyes locked with my blue-grays, and in that dreaded moment a decision was made on each side. His, was to push for me as far as he could; and mine, was to get out of there on foot.

He eventually won.

Time melted through the proceeding days, but I was not going with them. I had surface sensations to the skin and muscles, but couldn't move any of my limbs; they were leaden. Somehow I had become stuck in a horrible place, where terrible things were occurring, and I didn't have an ounce of independence. My individuality had been swallowed whole by an epidemic, which had spit me out as a number.

The more I thought about it, the madder I got. Was I ever going to get out of this condition, and if not, what then? I had never faced that question before, and didn't know how to use productively the heat of my anger.

In quiet moments my observations picked away at my budding journalist's mind. I dictated to myself two little paragraphs.

When your limbs don't respond anymore to remembered sequences of movement, you don't feel helpless, you feel terror. Panic crawls up your spine as you realize your mind is trapped in a useless body. A body on temporary loan. You begin to hate this body as though it's another creature outside yourself, and that if you had the choice you would discard it. After all, it had betrayed you.

It does not take long to see that the most simple actions, like scratching your nose, pulling hair away from your eyes, kicking the bedding, or holding a cup, are totally out of the question. At times you are afraid to try to move for fear it will be confirmed you can't. You continue to pray for the smallest motion, even lowering yourself to bargain with God.

More long days of laying immobile ground into restless nights. Then a strange phantom image appeared. I couldn't figure it out. She sat on the edge of my bed, donned my robe, and walked out the door. Finally it occurred to me it was my past self wrestling for freedom. She was the embodiment of my fondest desire—To walk.

Walking started to become an obsession.

Then I began asking anyone wearing a watch what time it was as though I had an urgency to be somewhere. In reality, I needed to place myself back in the normal scheme of things. One morning, very early, a small clock mysteriously appeared next to me while I slept. It came from Dr. Arzberg's apartment.

Finally, I used my time to develop a countdown list. The items on this mental list were the ten things I hated most: IVs, catheters, enemas, being naked under a sheet, being unable to eat and brush my teeth, too many hypos, no privacy, searing headaches, and, most of all, fear. As time moved forward I became amazed as the list got shorter. Dr. Arzberg was intrigued by the way my mind worked.

One dark night during a rainstorm, I awoke from the light of a flashlight held by another favorite nurse, Lois Jensen. She came in to check my temperature and pulse. Lois asked about the moaning sounds I had been making. She wondered if I were having more pain.

I replied, "I'm okay. The sound I make is a 'hum' noise. I use it to get in touch with my body, and it's comforting."

Lois patted my arm, "Honey, you use whatever works."

After she left the room, I had the first doubt that 'my warm light' that had appeared in my delirium had only been an ordinary flashlight, not a visitation. Was it only a hallucination, or could this be a testing of my faith? I didn't have an answer then for I was trying to cope with spiritual and physical collapse.

Although I couldn't see activity outside my room in the hall or go there, noises filtered through of the gasping iron lungs. Spending many hours breathing along with the wheezes, I willed all of the patients in the lungs to improve. It was hard for me to keep up with the mechanical pulse of the respirators, for it was not my natural breathing rhythm. I also started to think about others, especially after I learned that the man who had winked at me had died.

That bothered me for a long time.

Dr. Arzberg, on one of his late night rounds, stayed a while to talk. I welcomed the attention. He told me of a difficult patient they had had that morning. A young boy needed to be placed in the iron lung, and not only was he claustrophobic, but he fought the entire procedure. They solved the problem by taking him in and out until he got used to it, which showed him his stay in the lung could be changed.

Dr. Arzberg explained when they had mechanical troubles with the iron lungs they had to make quick transfers of the patients. The patients did not like it one bit, for they had become accustomed to their personal iron lung and were very proprietary. He said the move the patients did like was to have the machines shifted occasionally so they could have a different view. That view would allow them a glimpse of another face next to them, but yet one of the same ceiling.

Finally the daily patient count at the hospital started to decrease, and in this outpost extremely lucky ones walked away unscathed, many were left impaired, and some had died. Dr. Arzberg and I had become quite chummy, and he told me to call him Max whenever we were conversing alone.

Now that I was an insider, I got to know about everything that was going on in the hospital. Much of it was upsetting.

"Good," Max said, after I had given him an earful of complaints. He was looking for some fight in me, and that afternoon I moved my right hand an inch on the sheet.

A reward perhaps, and fearfully, would that be all?

At my pointed suggestion, which Max took graciously, he put music in the wards for the children. He saw to it they were given Kool Aid to drink, and that colorful bows and family pictures were stuck near the mirrors on the iron lungs. He liked the ideas, and I spent a lot of time thinking up a new one for him every day.

Later, fresh flowers appeared at nurses' stations, and paper cutouts of animals were hung from cribs. Along with the Illinois sunshine pouring into the rooms, there now was more luminous evidence of hope.

Nights were the longest times to get through, but I welcomed them, for the relative quiet and the moments Max visited. Even when I was half asleep I could feel his presense. When he came near I could smell the lotion he used on his hands, and when he leaned down to say something, I could catch a hint of his shaving cream. I never knew I could have such an awareness of someone.

Paul often came from the university to visit at the screen window. His junior year in architecture was starting with a full schedule, so he came when he had free time. Whenever he arrived, I was happy to see him, and tried to make conversation although I was in obvious misery. Most times he did the talking, telling me about his classes, his job as a junior draftsman in the architecture department, and news of our friends.

It was hard for me to see him standing out there, sometimes I resented it. I knew he was free to come and go, where I was acutely confined. Once he told me I looked just like a rag doll in my wool strips. Raggedy Anne.

Before he left, he said, "You know your situation is for a short time, and you'll be as good as new. You are not any different to me."

I clutched at those words like a lifeline for a long time, and that line eventually became my passage to the outside.

It's funny how the mind works. I am so furious I'm willing

to try anything, yet I'm completely paralyzed. What am I going to try? First I lose freedom of movement, then privacy, modesty, femininity, gracefulness, and identity.

I acted badly at first, for I tended to argue or not cooperate. No one here paid any attention. Although I have lost the title of being a normal person, I am now considered a Polio victim, with inferences of being maimed, crippled, impaired, lame, or handicapped.

How dare this happen to me, and why was I singled out?

Why has God let this happen?

I know I am beginning to learn about and maybe take on what I have become, mostly because I can't reverse it. It is a puzzle why I have skipped the grieving part, getting in there and wallowing in self-pity, but I figure I can do it later. As it turned out I never got around to it; recovery and urgency took over. Life had stepped in to hand me a burden and I could sink or swim.

The chafing question was, "Okay, so I'm alive, now what?"

My body soon became my teacher, as well as the staff that took care of me. I knew my legs were probably ruined, but not my mind. I had a few useful tools to explore and could put them to work, and leave the irreplaceable losses, the frustrations, and what my future might hold, to my soul. I didn't waste a moment thinking back about my life before becoming ill. It would be a crushing and painful reminder. Besides it was a futile exercise.

Had my youth fled with the onset of the disease, and had I matured overnight? Had I learned all this grown-up stuff from Max? Max had told me to use whatever tools I had, and had guided my thinking every day. He had really found the key to my intellect.

Gradual recovery from paralysis started to take place. The first tentative movement I attempted on my own was to bring my right thumb and forefinger together. Surprisingly, this enabled me to grasp a spoon. Getting food to my mouth was another matter, and sometimes it became quite funny.

I had started to eat solid food. It tasted metallic or medic-
inal, and I did not like it, but I was encouraged to eat anyway.
Finally, after a week of patience and practice to complete one
spoon-to-mouth connection, I succeeded. Although my victory was grand, I ignored the peas on the floor and the food
in my hair.

The odd part was, both my arms and hands did not work
the way I remembered. I could raise my head a little from the
pillow, but the whole process was exasperating and exhaust-
ing. My strength was definitely gone.

One evening, I mastered eating a cup of mashed potatoes
all by myself. Max heard my first laugh and dropped by to ask
me to comb my hair each morning and put on lipstick.

Clever fox.

Chapter 5

TALE OF DREAMS

Next on the schedule of events in the hospital was the arrival of four immunologists from Johns Hopkins Hospital in Baltimore, Maryland to study polio. Max asked if the team could interview me for an adult point of view. The doctors were introduced, and I was told they planned to correlate the details collected from this hospital with other information to help in their research.

Max, in a lighter moment, told the doctors that during a spell of delirium I had recited a calculus theorem, and it was right on the button. (I had taken an accelerated math course at the university.) He had kidded me, saying I was a real math scholar. I politely corrected him that I intended to be a journalist and would write books he would someday read. He told the doctors he believed me implicitly.

The Hopkins doctors asked about my lifestyle, where I visited, what I ate. They wondered what my ideas were on where I might have picked up the disease. I did not hesitate to answer: "Somewhere, I encountered contaminated milk."

Good guess, but probably not the right one.

Max stayed the whole time the men were in my room and I was comforted by his presence. I noticed I was always consoled by him, with his strength, his attention to detail, and by something else that conveyed itself through his eyes. That something I carefully avoided.

One evening about ten o'clock into the second week, Max casually strolled into my room carrying a nice red apple and a paring knife. He sat on a chair next to my bed and slowly peeled the luscious apple. He fed thin slices to me while he talked about this hospital being the hardest position he had ever held.

"I am only able to help my patients live," he explained, preparing another slice of apple, "ease their pain, while I am without a cure."

I felt an impulse to touch his hand, but held back.

"You're a wonderful doctor, Max, everyone here loves you. We're all getting the best of care and the best from you.

How can you ask any more of yourself?"

Max vacillated trying to find the right words, but opted to say nothing. The conversation was veering into a personal avenue and we both knew it was stepping over the line in doctor-patient relations.

Max instead steered the conversation to other matters. "Your next station will be the city hospital, and Dr. Rochelle will be taking over your case. You have been in isolation longer than usual because of the acute onset of the disease and the long phase of needing hot packs. Your legs will soon be getting back more feeling, too."

I gave him a withering glance. Max suppressed a laugh shaking his head, knowing I doubted him. I noticed he had perfect teeth, and laughed or smiled with me, not at me.

His eyes twinkled as a new thought emerged, and he grinned as he said, "You know you can do anything, be anything, and go anywhere in your mind, just like I told you before. Right now, imagine we have arrived at a formal ball, and I am ready to swing you into a waltz. Can you picture that in your mind, and add to my story?"

I chuckled at this make-believe of his, since it had always been one of my favorite past times. We made up a fabulous story together in the next half hour, even down to the descriptions of my gown, something in blue chiffon, and it delighted me and relieved some of my anxiety.

Max moved the story along, "And now since we have been dancing for a while, why don't we go out on the balcony and view the stars? Isn't it a beautiful night? I can see the river shimmering."

During the whole time Max and I talked he wasn't called away once to see another patient. I would always remember his exact words and what they did for me. They were locked in my heart.

Awakening early the next morning, I turned my head toward the window and saw the morning mists settle into the grass. I vividly remembered what it felt like to walk barefoot in the dew and have the moisture between my toes. I almost cried. Would I ever feel that again?

Paul arrived that evening to hear my longing story about walking barefoot, and placed his palm on the screen and asked me to position mine there also. I reached up with my left hand supported by my right, and felt the warmth of his hand. We shared a quiet moment while feelings of love pressed through the screen.

Max, about to step into the room at that moment, retreated quickly. A nurse passing in the corridor was startled by the abnormally dark look on the doctor's handsome face.

Inside the room I was unaware of the emotions I had created, and instead wondered if Paul thought I was worthy of love.

Someone else already did.

The week dragged by and the time neared for me to leave. All that was going with me was a small box holding the radio, comb and brush, and the clock Max told me to keep. I was afraid of all the new experiences ahead of me, and wanted to cling to those people I knew and trusted. Also, I didn't want to adapt to new hospital routines.

Max came for me along with two ambulance attendants pushing a wheeled gurney. I heard them coming down the hall. When they entered my room, Max instructed the men how to lift me, being especially careful of my legs.

As we moved out of my room, I slowly retraced with mixed emotions my trip down that corridor. I had a strong urge to sniffle, but kept it under control. Many came up to me to say, "Take care, and good luck." Lois and Lynn, who had spent most of the time with me, joined along on each side of the gurney until we reached the outside doors. Then the women squeezed my hands, and I thanked them for their special attention.

Once outside in the warm September air, I abruptly feel helplessly weak and exposed. Max reassured me by clasping both my hands in his, and reminded me that I was a survivor and could get through this change.

His hands trembled with emotion and I sensed alarm that we might embarrass ourselves out in this open driveway, and controlled yet another uneasy moment. What I really wanted to do was delay our parting.

Max climbed into the ambulance and saw that I was gently brought inside. There, he covered me tightly in a blanket, taking his time to tuck in all the loose ends. I attempted to thank him for the expert care he had given me, but he would have none of it.

He said instead, leaning close over me, "This is not the last you will see of me."

That cheered my heart, and he gave me a knowing wink.

I told him, "You know that I say prayers each night like you do. Well, a few were for myself, and I reminded God that I meant some of them to be retroactive."

Max reacted with a short laugh, got caught up in it as he left the ambulance, and I heard him chuckle all the way back across the driveway to the hospital.

I'm glad I made him laugh.

Chapter 6

❦

IS THIS ALL?

Champaign Gazette article:

POLIO PATIENT RELEASED FROM WARD

Polio continues to wane in this community, and no new cases in the county were reported in the 24-hour period ending Saturday noon. Miss Francy Holland finished the period of required isolation, and was transferred to Champaign City Hospital for further treatment.

With the ending of the eighth week of the community's polio epidemic several days ago, the sharp tapering-off trend was in line with predictions of district and local public health officers made earlier in the week. The wave is believed to have "run its course" for this season in the immediate locality, though two new cases in the county rural areas were reported and admitted for treatment at the polio hospital Friday morning.

Schools, meanwhile, were ready for the start of the fall term on Monday.

The epidemic was declared officially over on Thursday morning by Doctor C. F. Daniels, local health district officer, who then informed school executives to proceed with opening plans for this week.

Many children were not going back to school.

The ambulance ride turned out to be a nauseating, horizontal trip that had me reeling. I had no time or thought about being sad, apprehensive, or helpless. I spent most of the time trying to control my nausea.

I was relieved to arrive at my next unmoving "station." Max had told me the night before my departure that this would be a step up in my recovery. I learned the atmosphere here would be less forbidding, and found he was right as I was wheeled into a closed-off wing to a large room with big windows. The windows overlooked a pretty public park.

Alone in a new bed, I started to assess my condition. I could now use both hands. My back was unable to support me, and both legs were still useless. I could sit propped up by several pillows, and knew I had a long way to go before I could really help myself.

Okay, all in all, I may have never known before this illness about being tough or about survival, for I had a lot of emotional soft spots. But I did know that I didn't make it this far alone.

In spite of my sad assessment of short term gain and long term loss, I had a wonderful experience that afternoon. Two nurses, young, happy, and so willing to make my situation pleasurable, washed my long hair. They managed, with much laughter, to get my hair clean and dried, but the room and bed were a shambles. Water was everywhere, and both nurses' uniforms were soaked.

By the evening mealtime everything in the room, including me, had been transformed. Bedside lamps had been turned on, music poured from my radio, fall flowers appeared in vases for the first time, and I was promised strawberry ice cream for dessert.

When my first visitor arrived, I wore a new gown and robe, a pink ribbon in my hair, and was shining in more ways than one. I really felt like a new woman. When Paul happily rushed into my room and kissed me for the first time in four weeks, my heart raced with delight. I no longer felt like an invalid, and knew that I could accomplish just about anything. Paul somehow at that moment had the capacity to make me feel competent and loved.

He sat on the edge of my bed holding my hand radiating his delight that I looked so much better and not quite so bed-ridden.

"See, I told you you would get better. And although they still don't know if I could get polio from you, I'll still take the chance of holding and kissing you. After all, we were in each other's company when you were in the infectious stage."

I marveled at his words, thrilled that he wanted to be with me, but didn't want him to see my shriveled legs, or see all the things that had to be done for me. He, on the other hand, was very observant, noticed little changes, and encouraged me to try to move and get stronger.

Two weeks passed while I remained in hospital quarantine with only close relatives visiting. Undaunted, Paul continued to keep me up to date about the outside world. He did practically all the talking, going into great detail about what he was doing in school. Also, he had won the design contest sponsored by the *Chicago Tribune*. It seemed his future was on target.

Meanwhile, I waited passively to improve, trying not to worry about how much time it was taking. That was another matter, the keeping track of what day it was without a calendar. I had never thought about how dependent I was on many little things until I became vulnerable. I tried to not think about how frightening that was.

Dr. Arzberg came to visit several times, and on one occasion found me in a very sulky mood. We conversed for about fifteen minutes, and then he said, "You know, Francy, I have many patients to oversee. A little girl of four died this morning from polio at the isolation hospital, and there is no consoling her parents. Look around here, and you will see people a lot worse off than you. Remember this phrase, 'There, but for the grace of God, go I.'"

He's done it again. He is bringing me up short, and making me stretch beyond myself.

From then on I began to see where I fit in the bigger picture if I were ever to fit in it at all. I understood the meaning of the good fortune I had received. It became a turning point, of which there were many, but one that gave me a true sense of self-worth. Max had invested time and thought on me, and I was beginning to realize that he held me in high regard.

But the burning question was, where did *he* fit in the picture? He was so polished and educated, and he was a mature twenty-seven. I only dared for moments to think of him as a man, not as a doctor. That was most enticing but dangerous.

It was October, and all that could be done for me in the way of nursing had been tried. My doctors decided that I should go to Carter Hospital for convalescence.

I smiled when I learned of this next move. No one knew, but when I was ten years old, I had secretly trespassed the Old Carter Mansion, the one that later was converted into the convalescent hospital. Two friends and I had cooked up a scheme to sneak into the house to check out the ghost story I had made up about it.

It turned out to be a massive, spooky building of pink stone. Inside were mahogany paneled walls, huge model ships in cases on ornate credenzas, dense drapes on tall windows of stained glass, and rooms filled with elaborate furniture. Truly, it was not haunted, for a caretaker heard us giggle and came to scoot us out. We passed through a paneled door into the backyard. There we saw an empty swimming pool, maze gardens, and tall, serpentine brick walls. We were politely ushered out the gate.

I remembered statues of dolphins and mermaids around the pool. Now I was going to reside in that mansion. The saying that 'what goes around, comes around' is true. This past invader was going to return to the scene of the crime.

I arrived at Carter Hospital in the late afternoon via another ambulance, but sitting on an incline. The funny little phantom went with me.

This trip was more pleasant because I could view the colored autumn leaves all the way. The bonus was a drive through the downtown business district of Champaign, and I found everything was just as I had left it. Sobering thought: nothing had changed but me.

At the hospital a large outside paneled door was opened to an elevator, and I was whisked up to the second level. I was wheeled through the dim halls past private rooms with somber lights, upholstered armchairs, and heavy flowered drapes. This hospital had an atmosphere of elegant peace and quiet.

Too quiet. Have I been transferred here to die?

When settled in and again alone, I realized I was still bedridden and trapped in a room on a second floor. I immediately thought of fire. I made a plan of what to do in an emergency, and realized for the first time I was taking control of what was going to be the outcome of my stay.

How many firsts there are. Where is Max when I need him?

Max was at that very moment speaking in person to Dr. Donald Rochelle, an orthopedic surgeon. The surgeon would be continuing to monitor my case, but this time at Carter.

Soon two roommates were wheeled into my room. Joyce and Alice were from outside the county. Both were in their mid-twenties, had mild cases of polio, and could freely move around. My bed position was in the middle, and I was the only one bedridden.

Joyce, Alice, and I were a lively threesome most days, and our laughter dispelled the gloom of our combined conditions. Joyce had a lovely singing voice, and sang to us in the evenings. Alice was from a distant farm, and her people brought fresh food for many of our meals. Alice also has two jugs of cider under her bed, and one of them turned to applejack. We all had one jolly illegal evening. I'm sure our laughter could be heard clear down the hall to the first floor.

Needless to say, we didn't need any medication.

On Halloween night, my parents arrived dressed in costumes. My mother was dressed as a black cat with a long swinging tail, and my father was costumed as a hobo. They decorated our room with cutouts, and visited all the other patients on the floor, dispensing cider, doughnuts, taffy apples, and popcorn.

The nurses, and the head nurse, a former female sergeant in the army, spent a lot of time in our room in my four-month stay. I discovered I could be quite a storyteller with a droll sense of humor. I maintained from then on that humor would be the element that would save me. As long as I could see the bizarre, the ridiculous, and the ironic in life, I could make it.

My two roomies left for home one bright autumn day, and a new wrinkle came into my life. Dr. Donald Rochelle finally put in an appearance. We did not hit it off well on our first meeting. His authoritative manner and cool tone of voice stung. I was used to Max. Dr. Rochelle decided I was uncooperative, and I decided he was arrogant. His whole manner drove me to the edge of revolt, and I began to resist everything he wanted to do.

The next day what I heard outside my window as I ate an early morning breakfast was teeming life. Men in cars going to work braked at the cross-street, and children on the way to school skipped and dawdled, their piping voices rising to the second floor. A flash of resentment overtook me, and I choked on the toast. My world was not the way I wanted it. I wanted to be outside doing normal things.

Wishing would not make it so.

Dr. Collins came to visit later that morning, and I was surprised to see him. With my arms crossed over my chest I asked him why he had not come to see me earlier. He smiled at my impertinence.

"I have been checking on you through your other doctors all the while. You were and are in excellent hands. But I've come now in person to see you and settle an impasse."

I still was not mollified, and pleaded with him to be my attending physician or to send for Max. He smiled at me, breaking his stern demeanor.

"It is not my place to interfere with your treatment, Francy, and Dr. Rochelle is excellent in his field. Will you try harder to please, cooperate, since it is for your betterment?"

Chastised and warmed by his attention and concern, I agreed.

Max came for a visit that night after my evening visitors

left. There was a spring in his step and something was on his mind. This raised my spirits.

Seems all the men in my life are seeing me today. Word must have gotten out I am hard to handle.

I took some satisfaction in the fact that I had power to move people even though I was stuck in a bed.

Max saw that I could now sit up and shift my position, and expressed his delight by applauding as he approached my bed.

I knew the nurses found him handsome and interesting, for they kept coming into and out of the room for one thing or another during his stay. He soon became anxious to tell me something, and I sensed this. I smiled at his consternation, not really realizing how severe it was.

Max had brought me a calendar and some creamy mints in a black and gold foil box, and sat near me in an armchair eating the mints.

He said, "I've moved back to Central Hospital now that the isolation hospital is closed, and I prefer the easier pace. I have had a few interesting cases, and the hospital has some teaching classes for me. Those I like very much. Maybe that is my real calling."

I felt oddly close to him. We had shared a lot, we had history. I would have liked to have crawled into his lap and been hugged in comfort, and hugged him back, for at that moment he looked so open to expressing himself.

A strange tension quivered between us. Max had to bank his, I was bewildered by mine.

"By the way," he said, breaking the tension, "I agree with your doctors' verdict. Cooperation is necessary if you are going to move on to the next stage. You're good at this, and I expect you will see some interesting results."

"Yeah, well, sounds like a conspiracy to me, all you doctors getting together," I said with some pique.

"Of course we do. We are all concerned, and want the

best for you. You're not going to just lay there and molder. You have a lot of hard work ahead of you. And I will be there to help, I'm not abandoning you."

Later when he stood up to go, I was disappointed he was leaving, but encouraged by his words.

Max took my hand in his, and with a husky voice said, "Remember, Francy, you are still my prize patient. I expect great things from you."

"Yes, I know that, and I couldn't bear to disappoint you."

When he left, I wondered what was really on his mind. I was still afraid to know. Maybe I was just imagining things, and this visiting me was all there was to it.

Chapter 7

❦

MERMAIDS

The next day I grudgingly gave in to Dr. Rochelle's wishes, and he prepared to put casts on my legs. I disliked the casts, but kept silent and did not let my feelings show. Instead, I fumed inside.

The casts were joined in the back, and when dry were bivalved (the tops were cut so they could be lifted off). I had been having agonizing spasms that stretched muscles in my legs and feet, that caused the muscles to constrict. Often the nurses would have to apply massage to relax my stiffened limbs. (This procedure of rigid splints was done to align my feet and legs in the correct position, relieve the spasms, and keep my legs from shortening.)

I had to stay in the casts for two whole weeks of straightening torture, with only occasional breathers, and it was very painful. It was a test of endurance and supreme sacrifice that I had let Dr. Rochelle have his way. I could not find anything funny to think about during the whole time, but I would not disappoint Max.

After the cast procedure was over, I lay in bed with my feet pressed tightly on a vertical footboard and thought. Tragedy happens every day, but not to me. What had happened wasn't a tragedy, but a misfortune. It found me and challenged me. Knowing how to survive is one issue, doses of cooperation are another. They both use the intellect. With humor, one eventually gets one's way.

Ha, I acknowledged, I've found a tool I like.

I became, without knowing it, a lot of different people throughout this siege that rearranged my thinking. What were my priorities, and could I focus on them? The upshot of all that mind bending was, that I carefully allowed positive people to lead me. I made a very conscious decision to move forward, no matter what.

As November approached, I made a sign to be put on the wall over my bed that read, 'Do not distoib, and close the door.' Independence was crawling back in. I also started to think about ways of getting out of that tiring bed.

Alone one day, I rolled over the edge of my bed into a large wooden wheelchair. Small wonder I didn't fall on the floor. Once settled in the chair, I figured out how to move about and left my room. Soon I rolled into a large marble bathroom.

A nurse found me studying the bathtub. I was trying to figure out a way to take care of myself. A bath had to be the ultimate.

We worked out the logistics, and it took two more nurses to lower me into the tub. I shook with weakness from my efforts, and felt a little queasy, but had no intention of telling anyone.

I heard the snap of the bathroom door closing and had the first moment of privacy in many months. Now I could look my body over like a mother examining her newborn. Ten toes, but I couldn't wriggle them. My left foot sort of dangled off to the right and I couldn't pull the foot up. My knees appeared the same, but my legs were very skinny. I barely had hips.

The hot water with lavender scented bath salts was divine, and I moved my legs from side to side. Interestingly, they floated. I leaned forward and added more water until it was over my waist. I stayed alone in this bath paradise in the luxurious bathroom until my skin wrinkled. I scrubbed myself clean, relaxed, and somehow healed inside as a woman. Little Miss Phantom slipped down the drain.

Brushing aside my weakness, I addressed how I was going to manage more independence. If I could use the bathroom in private, I could wash my hair, rinse out undies, and do all sorts of things. Not much would have to be done for me!

Max was always pushing at the back of my mind.

On a fine late November day, about dinnertime, Paul drove to the hospital to pick me up. He had a big grin on his face, and eyes full of mischief. He had a mission. He lifted me into the wheelchair, wrapped a pink robe and a warm blanket around me, and sped us down the corridor to the elevator.

The elevator lowered us to the first floor and to the door to the outside driveway. In the cold night air Paul's car awaited.

We drove away from the hospital toward a fast-food drive-in, while I reveled in my getaway. I ordered real french fries and a chocolate milkshake!

Having been sprung, I was deliriously happy. Paul was proud of his idea, and kept looking at my face absorbed in my joy. It was fun to be alone with him and to be able to converse without others listening. He could also kiss me as much as he wanted which was getting a little dangerous. His access to me through my nightgown was thrilling, setting me on fire.

Before getting sick, I had known a small part about the workings of my own body. Now I knew volumes. Passion had blossomed before, boldness had taken over, and I hadn't known where it was headed. Paul did, and kept it in check.

After our meal we took one of our favorite drives out in the country. We had a serious talk while my cheeks flamed, and my whole body strained for him. I was ready to find out more about desire, and he knew it.

He became a patient and generous lover overcoming obstacles, treating me as most precious. He murmured words of love and assurance, and I snuggled in his arms knowing, trusting, and loving back.

No one had seen us leave, and a few anxious phone calls were made to discover where we might be. When we returned, and Paul wheeled me back down the corridor to my room, everyone seemed amused. I felt different as Paul picked me up and lowered me to my bed. His eyes locked with mine, and he whispered more words of love. He then possessively kissed me a sound goodnight. He nearly skipped out of the room.

Our escapade was talked about for some time around the hospital. The story was how a patient had been stolen away like a fairy tale princess by a prince on a white horse.

Nurses heart's are made of gold and unreserved romance.

When Max heard about our flight from the hospital of that

night, he banged his fist on his desk upsetting a full cup of coffee over the journal he was reading. This was going to gear him up for some positive action, let alone cleaning up the coffee.

The outpouring of kindness from acquaintances and strangers toward me was heartwarming, but I recalled the phrase, "Let a disaster strike, and you will find out just who your friends are." I knew in a short time who I could count on: those who treated me like they always had, and those who ignored my condition.

My usual day was hospital routine, meals, passive therapy, and an afternoon to myself. Since I also had artistic leanings, I spent many hours drawing with colored pencils, large, wickedly funny portraits. The doctors and nurses loved them. Although my psychological self was coming out on paper, most of the faces I drew were caricatures, and they assuredly represented the inner anger and unhappiness I was trying to hide.

One day I looked up from the face I was drawing and saw a stranger standing in the doorway watching me. He was tall, good-looking, had russet hair, was athletically built, and was neatly dressed.

I am always surrounded by attractive men. I wonder who sends them?

He advanced into the room with purpose walking like one who knew just how his body worked. "Hi, I'll introduce myself. I'm Bob Shelton. I'm a physical therapist at the university in the athletic department. I help injured athletes become rehabilitated. Your doctor, Dr. Rochelle, asked me to speak to you about trying some resistance therapy."

He smiled and changed his story, "Actually, I asked if I could see you. I had heard there was an adult female here who had polio."

I liked him immediately, and was overjoyed to hear there was another method of getting better. Bob explained that resistive therapy was a new therapy and that he would have to get permission from my parents to work with me.

When he called them, he was invited out to the house. One sterling comment Bob made to me about my condition before leaving my room was, "I think I can put you on your feet."

Imagine how my parents will feel when they hear that! And Paul! And Max!

When Paul came that evening for a visit, he was delighted to hear about the new program and said before he left the room, "When you can walk to the door, we will get married."

Wow! My cup was remarkably full that day, for this was a tall order. I would have jumped for joy, if only I could, but instead hugged myself in bliss. When I told the nurses, they became all-a-buzz.

I gave myself a year to overcome all the hurdles.

Bob arrived the next day with Dr. Rochelle to learn just how much damage to my body polio had caused. I had smug satisfaction that the two men were oddly restrained toward each other. They made charts, conferred, and asked me to attempt movement in feet and legs. They saw that I could wiggle the toes on my right foot, had faint activity in the left, and could move my legs a little to the side.

Besides that, although I had skin sensations, and anyone touching my legs brought pain, everything from the waist to the ankles was barely active. When they were finished with their examination, I hurt all over and expressed it.

Bob took my hand in his, patting it reassuringly. "The pain is only the beginning, and the exercises I have planned will in time ease the discomfort."

The following day I wondered why everyone was in such a hurry. I soon found out that Bob was a mover and a shaker. He had also worked out a plan with the local YMCA to use their swimming pool for ten polio patients. We would have Thursday mornings to swim and play. I had been a strong swimmer before, and eagerly awaited the first plunge.

It turned out to be a fatiguing trip to the pool, and a lot harder than I ever imagined. My pretty bathing suit was difficult to put on, and negotiating the wheelchair around the pool area took a lot of strength. Once at the pool I realized I didn't know how to get out of the wheelchair and into the water.

Bob watched me figure it out. With a determined look on my face, I rolled the chair to the railing at the deep end, quickly pulled myself up on the two bars, dragged my two legs, and dropped down into the water.

I sank like a rock. I hit the bottom of the pool and quickly looked up to see a dozen moving feet. Although I could not push off from the bottom, as I used to, I managed to pull myself back up to the surface. Bob was there to grab me, laughing at my first attempt.

He showed me smoother ways to get into the pool and I was soon swimming freely. My strong arms reached out and pulled me along, but my useless legs trailed behind. Woefully, I had become a mermaid.

Bob worked with me for a half-hour therapy session, and then demonstrated water exercises I would be doing on my own when I got stronger.

I felt like a million in the buoyant water, and could finally be graceful and move freely. Bob knew I would find out eventually, but it was still a bit of a rude jolt to realize just what muscles worked and which ones didn't. The losses were permanent. No kidding myself there.

Max heard about the new skills and made an appointment with a jeweler. He asked him to find a gold mermaid charm and attach it to a chain bracelet. When the jeweler called back the next day to say he had found a mermaid and other associated sea charms, Max gave him the go ahead to make it.

Late one evening, after the hospital had quieted, Max arrived with his surprise. I was thrilled with each charm: three shells, a grass shack, a seahorse, and a mermaid.

Max fastened the bracelet hoping his gift had a claim to my heart.

"Max, you are a dear I shall treasure this forever, " I told him as I reached up to cup his face in my hands. "You are always first to congratulate me on my accomplishments, no matter how small."

As he bent toward me, I gave him a quick, friendly kiss, and he almost reached for me.

We chatted for about an hour, talking about what had taken place since his last visit. Then he saw I was getting tired. He stood near me, turning the bracelet around and around on my wrist as he said his goodbyes.

I squeezed his hand, smiling. "When will I see you next?"

"Soon," he assured me, "and remember, that to me you are special."

Everyone who saw the charm bracelet in the following days thought it was quite beautiful. Even Paul thought so, and in private, wondered if the gift had more meaning than he had at first thought. But having the confidence that I loved him, he soon put even that thought away.

Chapter 8

❧

INSIDE OUTSIDE

As another month passed, Bob became anxious to get me released from the hospital and into my room at home. There we could work every day. He felt I needed to start a hard regimen, and should be in a normal environment if ever I was to be independent.

Although I may have been delighted to be under the care of an expert trainer, I found out that the outside world was not quite ready for me. I weighed ninety-nine pounds, had very thin arms and shriveled legs, and was pale. I had seen veiled shock on other people's faces, but I had one best feature of my own: expressive, challenging blue eyes. Bob said that was where he saw the grit, and that made him want to work with me.

Finally my life was on an uphill climb, but the daily exercises were not a cup of tea. Bob told me jokes while he stretched the long-unused limbs. First we stretched, then we strengthened, and then we reeducated the muscles; it became a daily litany. Bob was a wonderful storyteller, and I laughed through my tears. He also confided that Dr. Rochelle was skeptical about this new therapy, and I now realized why they had locked horns.

One day Bob placed his hand over my right knee and pressed down. Then he said, "This is a type of therapy called, 'The Think Method.' I want you to first feel my hand, then think under my hand inside your knee. This could tighten your kneecap."

I thought he had to be kidding. With several tries, he said he thought he felt something. I was not ready to celebrate.

Christmas time arrived. The nurses helped me wash and set my hair, and I got to go home for three days. It took two attendants from the hospital to lift me in the wheelchair up the front steps of the house. When I arrived inside, our cat was suspicious of the wheelchair and all the funny smells I had brought home, and scurried away. But her curiosity got the best of her. She crept back and spied on me from underneath the dining room table for fifteen minutes, and then came out and jumped into my lap. I guessed Betty knew me after all and had decided to forgive me for being away so long. Although her weight hurt my legs, I stood the discomfort, for to hold her warm purring body was an unmeasurable joy.

My parents had planned a day of parties on Christmas Eve so that everyone could come and be with me. The young girls in the neighborhood came from one o'clock in the afternoon until three, and college friends came from three until six. Friends of the family, Dr. Max, Bob, and Paul and his parents, came for the evening.

Although delighted to see everyone, I still felt weak and not all that recovered. I sat in my wheelchair near the tall, bright Christmas tree watching everyone moving about.

Wearing a full-length red velvet skirt with a long-sleeved blouse in white, and black velvet slippers, I felt very regal. Paul had brought a gardenia for me to wear on my wrist, and Max saw to it that I had plenty of eggnog to drink. I was surrounded by all the men that mattered in my life, and loved every one of them, all in very different ways. That was the first time I realized there were many types of love.

Near the end of January, I was finally allowed to go home for good. I could get into and out of bed by myself, and into and out of the bathroom, all with the use of the wheelchair. Dr. Rochelle had not been ready to release me from Carter Hospital until I had perfectly mastered those skills. My right knee was starting to respond to therapy, and not only that, so was the left. I had learned the 'Think Method.'

Many from my church sent prayers my way. One Sunday the minister dedicated his radio broadcast to me. He also read on the air my letter to the choir, of which I had been a member, of how their music had helped and inspired me during my illness: my choral vanguard.

All the days and weeks soon piled into February, and Bob and Dr. Rochelle had a meeting of the minds. Dr. Rochelle was informed of the progress I had made and suggested I have a fusion of the knee and the ankle to give me a stronger left leg. When I realized I would have a permanently stiff leg, I refused the surgery.

The two men then agreed that two muscle transfers could be performed instead to give me a stable left leg. Since the left was the most damaged, and I couldn't lift my left foot up from the floor, a drop foot operation would be done to correct it. Although the surgeries are not guaranteed to be a complete success, they are at least warranted.

Max called to talk and encourage me about the surgeries, and I was disappointed not to see him. He was traveling a lot to seminars.

Through therapy as the weeks passed, my right leg, foot, and hip got stronger, and I began to show some muscle tone. My limbs at last had regained some shape. The thirty-five different exercises I received every day for the whole body took about two hours to complete. I was usually exhausted afterwards. Also I developed strong biceps in both arms from lifting my body weight into and out of the wheelchair.

The time finally came and Bob and Dr. Rochelle appeared in my room to measure me for full-leg walking braces.

Also, a pair of wooden crutches was brought in. They ended up resting in a corner. They silently reminded me they were for a walking person.

It took three weeks to make the braces, and Bob brought them out to the house. He was all excited, and rushed around getting me ready for my maiden voyage. My mother stood to one side watching the event. The cat headed for the basement.

The braces were pairs of steel bars topped by wide leather straps that would go around each thigh. The bars descended to the knee, where another set of leather straps was attached to hinges that locked. Then the bars sank to brown tie-shoes and another pair of hinges. I gave them a jaundiced eye when Bob stood them up on the floor near my chair.

He laughed at me, "Hey, don't look like that, these are your transportation."

The braces weighed about thirteen pounds apiece, squeaked, and when Bob strapped them on and helped me upright for the first time, the entire world tilted crazily. (It took weeks for my balance to stabilize.)

Bob pushed the new wooden crutches under each arm, and steadied me while I made a wobbly move. I didn't know what to do first.

How does one walk? What are the mechanics? I used to be so sure of where my feet were, how to point my toe in skating, and what balance it took to walk in high heels.

Feeling so awkward and dumb, I was also partly annoyed. I could not lift my foot and my knees were strapped in tightly, so I scooted one foot forward, and then a crutch as Bob instructed. I knew my mother was holding her breath while I negotiated my first stiff-legged step.

Walking like a robot wasn't so bad. I was vertical, on my feet, and moving. The local newspaper photographer, having been forewarned of this first attempt, arrived to take my picture. The caption over the photo in the evening newspaper read, "FRANCY STANDS!"

Betty came up from the basement, lured by the excited voices, and spent some time sniffing the new braces, paying particular attention to the leather straps. She took a long nap with me later.

When Paul came that evening to see the progress, he got tears in his eyes when he saw me stand. I realized I had forgotten how tall he was. When Max arrived, I marveled that the two men were equal in height. It was also the first time I noticed that the men seemed a bit antagonistic toward each other. My mother had caught a glimpse of it too.

Five new teenage friends in the neighborhood hung out at the house every chance they got. Somehow I had become their heroine. With each advancement in my ability, they took credit. My father had seen to it that parallel bars were installed outside near the back door, and every time I went outside to walk the bars, the girls would mysteriously appear.

In many ways they became my support network. I saw through them what I might become.

Not long after these events, I was brought up short by the Queen Bee Syndrome. I had been given the best of treatments, catered to with much personal attention, and had people at my beck and call around the clock. Then it all came to a halt. People went back to their busy routines, and I was left with my therapy sessions and a lot of time on my hands. Somehow I had been under the impression the attention was going to go on forever, that I was entitled.

The Dictionary told me: Entitle, Entitled, Entitling—to have a claim or right to.

Humility be thy name.

February blew in, icy and bright. The day before my twentieth birthday, two muscle transfers were performed on my left leg at Marshall Hospital. These were to strengthen my left foot and to enable me to lock my left knee straight so it would not collapse when I put weight on it. The operation on the left foot was for drop-foot.

Dr. Rochelle came to my hospital room with paper and pen. He settled in an armchair near me. Then he explained in detailed drawings how he was going to borrow a working muscle and stitch it to the area that did not work. He had done this often in the military to save knees and ankles of soldiers injured in combat.

Since my quadriceps, or knee extensors were paralyzed, the only muscles that were large enough and locally available for him to use were Hamstrings-knee flexors. Later, Bob would retrain the muscles to take over new tasks.

"When I do this transfer, you understand Francy, the strength of the muscle drops a full grade. That means in the normal/good/fair/absent grades. Your body has to retrain itself to realize that when it thinks to straighten the knee, it is now going to have to use a muscle group that was intended to flex it.

"The operation starts surgically exposing the hamstring

insertions on the back of the tibia. They are then tagged with sutures and cut off the bone. A tunnel is then made from the back of the thigh to the front. The cut ends are pulled through and attached with heavy sutures to the quadriceps just above the kneecap."

I was most impressed, and knew for the first time why Max and Dr. Collins had such confidence in Dr. Rochelle.

He continued, "This surgery is still being done in areas of the world with either polio or similar unchecked diseases. It could be done in a situation in which due to trauma, the quadriceps were torn away. Now when you have recuperated, Bob will retrain the muscles to take over their new tasks."

I knew the names of muscles as Bob had shown me a chart, and had told me the percentage of damage that affected mine. I had conflicting power; where one side was strong, the other was weak: hips, thighs, knees, and feet were opposites.

After the full-leg cast came off, I saw I had fifty-nine stitches along the left side of my left leg and across my knee and foot; I was proud of every one of my battle scars. Bob and I worked to get the transfers to do their job, and at first it was a bit confusing, for my muscles were doing something different from what they were initially intended. Eventually I got the hang of that too.

By late spring I was not falling down as much, but when I did, it usually sent Betty scurrying. The braces made a racket, and the crutches would spin away from me. But she would come back and rub her head against me as I sat on the floor as much to say, "It's okay, we all embarrass ourselves at some time."

I could get myself up from the floor at home by pulling myself gradually up the front of the sofa. I had taught myself all sorts of emergency measures.

Months passed and I was still struggling with the braces, crutches, and the wheelchair. I had nearly gotten over being stared at in public, and stared back. It took scads of emotional and physical energy to go out, and most times I dreaded it.

Paul knew this, and took me everywhere. By wheelchair, it was first excursions around the neighborhood, and then to a football game at the U. of I. Stadium. Paul learned all about how the hinges of the braces worked, how to adjust the crutches, and how to spin the wheelchair until I was screeching for mercy.

Later he was able to get me into the ice rink, a special treat, to see the show "Holiday on Ice." Paul carried me from the wheelchair to my seat, and tucked a blanket around me.

I had skated on this very rink since I was five years old in tiny black figure skates. My father said when I learned to skate backwards and could stop, I would get a pair of white skates. I got them the next year. I enjoyed watching the skaters, particularly studying their legs and feet, really wanted to be out there with them, but knew I never would.

A segment in the middle of the show ended with a clown act. When the spotlight bathed him in an extra bright glow, he skated over to where we were sitting and leaned over to hand me a lovely long-stemmed red rose. I was very touched by the gesture, and wondered who had told I would be here. I thought it might have been Max. It was his style. But when he visited me at home, he denied it. He would.

When I reached the age of twenty-one, as though it was a gift, the right brace was made into a half-brace or short-leg brace. Bob promised I would be tossing away the left brace before long. He said my progress was miraculous, and that I had made incredible strides.

I had found out that a trainer using resistive therapy could get me as far as I could go, and I had many places I wanted to go. There were abundant new tears during these times, however, sometimes because of emotional struggles and other times because of physical ones. Most of them never reached my face, though. They landed on my soul.

Chapter 9

✢

STEEL RODS

In June I was offered a job to edit and write for the college paper, *The Orange and Blue*, which became a new step in confidence. My bosses were not hesitant to hire a handicapped woman, and were the first ones on campus to do so. I was delivered by car each day by my father, and handled the eight hours of work just fine.

Working with normal people all day, I found I was accepted. I made new friends and learned to use the IBM machines. This was my first exposure to accuracy, and I loved the challenges.

One day on campus, when I walked back to the office after lunch, a large Saint Bernard, called Bernie, mascot of the Sigma Chi fraternity, latched onto one of my crutches and ran down the street with it. He had people chasing him for blocks, and some people on the sidewalks had to dodge the happily cavorting dog with his long stick. His owner was very apologetic when he brought back the crutch—with teeth marks. I then became leery of dogs; at least Bernie hadn't lifted his leg.

My worst fear was falling down at work. In the stockroom one day getting a few papers, the uneven floor tripped me up. I sat on the cold concrete floor waiting for someone to come help me. I wondered if I would have to sit there until five o'clock. Finally someone came in and got me up on my feet.

At the gym after work, I told Bob. He wasn't happy about my predicament. He set to work teaching me how to get up by myself from a floor-mat, and how to walk up and down stairs. I hadn't been aware of so many hazards in public before, and hadn't yet been out in ice and snow. Curbs I could handle, and getting into and out of a car; it just took more time.

Athletes working out at the gym who had been injured in sports events, showed a lot of respect for my efforts. They would sometimes stop what they were doing to watch the method I used to get up from the mat.

Out in public, I had learned to look people straight in the

eye without flinching, but sometimes some could not look back.

Did they feel guilty that they had been caught staring? Were they feeling pity they did not wish me to see? Or were they thankful my problems were mine and not theirs?

Paul was in his fourth year of architectural studies, and our destinies were moving closer. Whereas my plans were on hold indefinitely, ours were charging ahead. Paul also didn't feel in the least threatened by attentions other men gave me, for he felt I was his.

What were my plans before all this happened? I couldn't remember.

Max phoned me at work. We made plans to go to dinner that evening, and I didn't think it a bit out of the ordinary to go with him. In fact, I was thrilled he had finally asked. My parents thought it was very nice Max had invited me. I didn't explain it to Paul knowing he would object.

Was that the real reason?

Max picked me up at the office in his new gray Mercedes, and we drove to a place specializing in Italian food. I admired the car and the fine leather upholstery. Max was very attentive and took charge of our orders when we reached the restaurant, selecting a full-bodied red wine to go with dinner.

We truly enjoyed each other's company and talked avidly about work, classical music, and what books we were reading. When our meal was finished, we went outside into the night air, marveling at the balmy weather and being together. Max carried my coat and guided me to the car. He then asked, "I have a newly decorated apartment and would like to show it to you. Will you come?"

With part excitement and part hesitation, I agreed. We would be alone in his home.

As we wound through the streets on the way to his apartment I wondered why I had feelings of guilt. I wasn't doing anything wrong, nor was Max.

Once inside his apartment, I looked around, admiring the

wonderful colors and placement. He had black and white leather furniture in nice groupings, scarlet Oriental rugs, and very contemporary lighting near chairs. A tall round column of clear glass to one side of the living room caught my attention. It rose to the ceiling, and inside the glass were colored shells and sea creatures made of wood that spiraled upward and moved on invisible wires. I was captivated by the display.

He was pleased with my reaction.

Max turned on some music while I read titles on his bookshelf moving about the room. "Will you have wine?" he asked, coming near me.

I declined as I was already spinning with pent-up emotions. Why do I feel this way? What do I sense between us?

When we seated ourselves on the couch, savoring the fine music, Max reached for the blue velvet box he had placed earlier on the glass coffee table.

He placed it in my hands. I turned to him with a puzzled expression. "Max, what is this? You mustn't spoil me with more gifts."

He urged me to open the box and dispel the suspense, and I saw that something else was at play in his eyes.

Inside the jeweler's box coiled a pale pink necklace of matched pearls. The clasp was made of a circlet of diamonds surrounding an amethyst. A card tucked in the back of the box described the necklace. I couldn't read the words, for my eyes were filled with futile and regrettable tears.

"Don't cry, Francy," Max urged, as he took the card from my hand. "The card reads, 'One Hundred and One Pearls of Love.' They are yours, no matter what. I'm just trying to help you decide."

In anguish, I closed the box on the lovely treasure sadly shaking my head. I returned the box to his hands. I rose, took hold of my crutches, and started to walk to the door. My hand was on the doorknob when he stopped me. He stood behind and gripped my shoulders steadying me, and pulled me back against his chest.

I had never been in his arms before.

He buried his face in my hair and pleaded, "He can't have you, he doesn't deserve you. He's not right for you. Believe me I know."

I placed my hand over my mouth to keep from sobbing, and the tears continued to spill down my cheeks. When he turned me around, I refused to look up for fear he would try to kiss me, and knew if that happened I would be lost. I might surrender. I had made my choice, but still wasn't sure it was the right one.

Wordlessly we drove to my house. At the door, I gave Max the key to open it. When he firmly placed the key in my hand, I looked into his face for some answers. But there were none, or else he couldn't put his feelings into words. He kissed my cheek, returned to the car, and slowly drove away. I closed the door behind me, tormented by the evenings events.

Oh Max, I thought, as I hung my coat up in the closet. Something was in one of the pockets, and I drew out the blue velvet box. He was going to haunt my sleep. He had such ties to me. He had declared his love. Now the gift was another. I fitfully dreamed and cried all night.

Paul called early the next morning, cheerfully reminding me we were going on a picnic with friends. I spent the day alternating between feelings of guilt and regret. Paul wanted to know why I looked tired and why my eyes were so puffy. I brushed away the question by explaining I had slept badly.

But later I decided perhaps I was right not to let Max become further involved. However, the attraction I had for him was seductive and different from the one I had for Paul. I owed both men a lot. I reasoned that time would quiet the ache.

My heroes.

That Christmas I received a surprise engagement ring from Paul. He had carefully wrapped it in tissue and placed it at the end of a long cardboard tube. My parents, in on the secret, had a cooled bottle of champagne in the refrigerator. Friends arrived to celebrate, and we had a party to remember.

At eleven o'clock we departed for the midnight service at church, and there I watched my ring sparkling in the candle-light as I listened to the choir acclaim, "Hallelujah."

Being engaged gave new stature to my life, and with it came a shiny pair of crutches. Since my back supported me well when I walked, I could hang up the wooden ones. The new canes were called Canadian crutches, having been developed there. They were hollow aluminum rods with metal hand grips and bracelet bands. The bands encircled the arms just below the elbow, and the hand grips jutted out from the sticks. These lightweight aides were adjustable, and the holes in the sides where they could be adjusted whistled different tunes when I was out in the open. I was never with-out an orchestra.

Chapter 10

❦

DANCING ON ICE

One afternoon, out of the blue, Max placed a call to my office. He had a problem he thought I could help him solve. He was all business. Carefully he explained he wanted me to come to the hospital Saturday morning and walk through a ward composed of men in varying stages of paralysis. I was to greet each man, and then leave.

Pay-back time for the Queen Bee.

Prior to my visit, Max told the men about my history. He was ready for me when I arrived, and I walked with him down the corridor of the hospital, he matching his steps with my slow ones. I knew he was just about the most important man in my life. I loved him in a way I could do nothing about. It was a quandary.

Max had something he wanted to discuss with me, and we headed for his office. He closed the door, took my crutches, placed them near his desk, and helped me settle into an armchair.

"Would you like coffee?" He asked, watching me compose myself.

I declined by shaking my head.

"Good thing," he suddenly laughed. "When I heard the details of that night escapade of yours to the drive-in, I banged my fist so hard on this desk, I upset a full cup of coffee all over the journal I had been reading. Cleaning up the coffee spills cooled my anger at Paul for putting you at risk."

I hadn't known his feelings then and felt uncomfortable with his admission. He didn't know that night had changed my life.

"Anyway, the reason for your visit. I've been thinking about the public lives of the handicapped," he started. "Returning vets, amputees, others in wheelchairs or using crutches, have no voice concerning their care or how they will live their lives. They are sometimes completely ignored. Many times the family has to take on the entire burden. What I'm getting at is they face as you do, rejection, stares, overt curiosity, and all sorts of things that put them apart from society. They become peripheral. Do you understand?"

"Is that like peripheral vision, from the side?" I asked, not quite knowing where he was leading.

"What is closer is, society can't accept those who are not normal. Cruel, but true. They place the handicapped on the outside."

"Oh, I know where you're going with this. My bout with polio has shown me how I am treated now, opposed to how I was looked at before. Yes, there is a decided difference. I was once really angry with the injustice, the prejudice, but saw that humor and indifference to it could get me through. But it still hurts," I said with a tentative smile. "I know it will be with me the rest of my life in some form."

"What can we do about it?" he continued, trying to keep to the subject. "I've been asked to do some articles for the medical journals. Would you be willing to give me your input? And be willing to be involved? I know you are still giving blood for research, but this is something different."

"Yes, that would be wonderful. I have been wanting to write something, and this gives me an opening. We can't let any of this crusade to help slip by. You are a dear to want my help, and not with just today. You have been my champion all along, and I'm flattered by your regard."

And I said with a twinkle of knowledge, "I am not worthy of all the loving-kindness you have shown me."

He picked up on my statement immediately, being the Bible scholar he was.

"Ah, you have been going over Genesis. Good for you. Now I have a line to recite, but not from the Bible. It's something Mandell Creighton wrote: 'No people do so much harm as those who go about doing good.' Have you heard the saying, 'Beware the do-gooders?'"

"Yes, it sounds familiar," I admitted, trying to remember where.

"Well, that's another topic we need to discuss. There are people who prey upon those in need, trying to 'save' them.

They use them for religious reasons to make money. You may run across somebody like that one of these days. Be prepared, be courteous and use firm control.

"And as for not being worthy, you are, and the loving-kindness is for life."

Max shrewdly studied Francy, knowing she was very aware of him. He wasn't kidding himself and thought—she is all tied up in conflict, and I'd like to take advantage of it, but won't. There are times I think she can't handle all she has taken on, and I'd like to step in and take over. Shield her, take care of her. Other times I remember her grit, stubbornness, and the willingness to laugh in the face of opposition, and know she will be fine. She is noble, and brave, and I'll hold her in my heart forever. Without knowing it, or even having a purpose, her mission in life is to haunt my dreams.

"Okay," Max said rising from his chair. "I want you to meet the men in the paralytic ward. They are angry with what has befallen them, they are uncooperative, and some are bitter. You could make a difference."

I stood up, wondering if I were up to this task. I would never knowingly let Max down. As he handed me my crutches, I sensed so much between us and felt light-headed.

How I wish I could love him. If only I lived two lives. I know a little about attraction, but the way he feels about me, and the way he makes me feel, is more than attraction. I just don't know what it is. If he ever made another move, I would be lost. He has power and strength of purpose over me, and I would go spinning. I know I could never handle it.

We walked to the ward and Max introduced each man as he ushered me around the room. Eight pairs of eyes watched my every step and looked into my face as I spoke to each of them. Questions were asked, and the men seemed happy I was there. Max watched me all the while.

The men were just as hungry to walk as I had been.

"How long were you bedridden? What did it feel like to take your first step? What was the worst hospital experience?

Who helped you the most? Will you get any better?"

I answered each truthfully. "I was bedridden for six months. In hospitals for a year. My first step was frightening, I couldn't remember how. I ended up walking like a robot."

That got a laugh.

"The worst hospital event was being readied to go into an iron lung. However, Dr. Arzberg tried other methods to help me breathe. They worked, and I didn't have to go in. Guess who helped me the most?"

They all looked at Max.

"Yes, I'll improve by continuing my resistive therapy, I'll get stronger, but I'm walking as well as I ever will. I will always need crutches, but it's a small price to pay for mobility and independence."

I looked at Max for confirmation, and he nodded.

When I left and reached the outside hall to wait for Max, I heard him say, "Okay, you've seen the woman I told you all about. Isn't she something? Not one of you was hit as hard as she. Think about it."

He came out to thank me, picked up my left hand to look at the ring, his warm hand holding me still, and shook his head.

"So, it's official," he said in a tone not quite like him, almost a scoff.

We parted once more with unsaid words. The ache was still there.

Max called a week later to tell me the men in the ward became more enthusiastic about their therapy and recovery chances; my little walk-through had made a difference.

I felt proud that Max had needed me as much as the men. During that year, I also helped Max with written material for his medical papers. All business of course.

When I turned twenty-two, improving myself had become my life's work. Was I going to be normal or abnormal, what image did I want to present, could I get away with normal? I was becoming a careful observer and my eyes were opened to the subtle nuances of expression in people. Finding there was power in observation; it fed my ego, achievement satisfied my mind, and regard nourished my heart. I learned to shield myself and to insulate personal feelings. When something serious needed deliberation, I could focus.

Did I learn that from Paul or Max?

One revealing aspect about my encounters with people confirmed that some could not handle being around the handicapped. Children, however, were always curious and had no fear. They would come up to me with big, shining eyes, take hold of one crutch, and ask, "Why do you have these? Did you get a boo-boo? Can I try them?"

I usually explained I had been ill, my legs were weak, and I needed them to help me walk. "Oh," would be their comment. They were always satisfied with my answers. The most common remarks I heard from adults were, "Oh, I know just how you feel. I was on a pair of those for six weeks with a broken leg." The next was a question, "Was it an accident?" or, "Tell me what I can do to help."

The friends that came into my life and stayed were carefully watchful and helped only when needed. They did not appear randomly. They were sent, for there are angels working diligently just about everywhere.

Whether I wanted it or not, my character became more defined, and I emerged as a symbol with the responsibility to carry it well. I soon discovered I took on too much, and had another learning school to attend for stamina, energy level, and health. Sometimes trying to be 'normal' got ahead of me, and I paid for it by having to back off. I spent too much time trying to match pace with everyone.

Somewhere in all of this, I had left my youth behind, and overnight I had become an adult. The things I missed most were running up the stairs, cycling, ice skating, and walking with Paul through the autumn leaves on star-filled nights. We liked to walk everywhere.

Are our dreams told in the stars? I liked to think so.

The white figure skates hanging in my closet and the sling-pumps with two-inch heels I had once bought were constant reminders of another person and another life. One day the shoes and skates were put in a box in the basement next to the red bicycle that sat on flat tires.

"Well," I promised myself, "I can't get back all I lost, but I'll be content with getting back some of it."

The bigger portion, that is.

I was improving and didn't know at what level it would end, so I nudged my eagerness and enthusiasm to expand. This encouraged people around me to ignore the fact I was handicapped.

Some forgot it entirely, which amazed me.

I still had the need to educate people to my wants, and never step over the line of letting them do too much for me. It was a fine balancing act, and most times it worked. Limits were there each day, and I knew I'd never learn to pace myself. I had a very active mind; it was always two steps ahead of my body. The recovery time did come to an end, but I never noticed.

Occasionally black hole moments descended, when my mind sank to a level where the sins dwell. These could not be easily shrugged off. Envy, jealousy, resentment, paranoia, all sorts of problems reared their ugly heads to prod. More of the devil's work. My emotions still yo-yoed, and I struggled to get them under control, for this new person was intriguing and I found it a great source of satisfaction to try her out.

Many of our friends had married, and Paul and I went out often to dinner and to sports events with them. The couples learned to tailor these outings to make it easy for me, for there were not many places that I could go unless there was a ramp, elevator, or on-grade entrance. Sometimes I was carried, one time to a downstairs voting booth. I tried to not think of those times as humiliating, but enabling.

I knew I would never dance again, but Bob, 'Never say I can't', proved me wrong. He and his wife invited Paul, my parents, and me to his club for a Saturday night dinner dance. He pulled me up out of my chair and onto the dance floor. I protested, but he would have none of it, and led me into easy, sliding steps. He knew when to give support to my left side and glided me smoothly around the floor while Paul seethed. It was not long before Paul was on his feet coming to claim me, and Bob showed him how to help. Bob chuckled all the way back to our table.

Paul whispered in my ear, "I can't bear to see you in any man's arms."

After the maiden voyage on the dance floor, Paul decided to take me to a formal ball at his fraternity. I hurriedly called one of my best friends, and explained my desperate need for a formal. She arrived with the perfect dress. How had she known? It was a cream-colored silk, full-skirted and banded in wide black lace. It had an off-shoulder bodice.

The night of the dance I was so excited I could hardly contain myself. I donned the slippery dress, tied a thin black velvet ribbon around my neck, and put on black velvet slippers. Paul arrived with a creamy gardenia to complete my attire. He was exceedingly handsome in his tux, and my heart fluttered with love.

Max drove up as we left the house, having been invited for dinner by my parents. Gallant as always, he complimented our formal attire with approval. His eyes held something more, and he told me he would call soon. Paul was in a snit all the way to the dance.

I could easily have been deluded that no one paid much attention to the fact that Paul was engaged to a handicapped woman, but in truth, I stuck out like a sore thumb. I was also the only noticeably disabled person on campus.

However, that same year a building at the university was outfitted with ramps and handrails. Returning war veterans (paraplegics), could now come in wheelchairs and engage in studies and sports. But I was still the only handicapped woman there.

Chapter 11

❧

CHOICE MADE

The year started with my being given a raise at work, and taking two correspondence courses at the university in journalism. Paul would be graduating soon, and going off somewhere to complete a military obligation. We had a few stiff arguments about plans for the future, and when I attempted in exasperation to remove my engagement ring, Paul quickly amended his stance.

"I really wanted to wait for marriage until I graduated and got my military obligation over. But I don't want to lose you, because if I proceed on my own, Arzberg or someone else will move in. There are men out there who want to protect you and are falsely attracted, Francy."

He took my hand in his, urging me closer. As I looked into his earnest face, I thought I was going to hear more words of caution and denial. Instead what I heard was, "Be mine, Francy. Will you be my wife? I promise to care for you, protect and love you. We can marry in two months when I am between semesters. Will you?"

On a smoldering kiss, I breathlessly said, "Yes."

Events started to fly pretty fast as we began the countdown with preparations for a wedding. Everyone in our immediate circle was nervous about how in the world we could possibly pull off having a normal life. We didn't have a clue ourselves, but were willing to brave the obstacles, being reminded of the line about 'stepping in where angels fear to tread.' For some reason we were confident the angels were on our side.

Max didn't think so.

We were to be married in the chapel at my church, the Episcopal Methodist. I found a sky-blue lace gown in a smart downtown shop, and made my own veil from matching net. I intertwined the headband with pearls and gathered the rest into a circular shoulder-length veil. My low-heel pumps had to be dyed the color of my dress, and one of our ushers took care of that chore.

The glorious day finally arrived on the heels of an ice

storm. Paul bravely carried me across the slick street from his car while his parents looked on. My parents and guests also made their way gingerly following us. Paul slipped once, but got his footing, and held me tighter for the rest of the way.

Safely inside, Paul was greeted by the best man and the ushers, and herded away. I heard the organ playing softly as my mother and I retreated to the church parlor to ready my veil, and for the photographer to take a few pictures.

Now, for the most important steps of my life. My Mother handed me my maternal grandmother's Bible wrapped in white velvet topped by the white orchid Paul had flown in from Florida. The organ sounded the first chords of Mendelssohn's wedding march, and my father took me down the short aisle to the slow cadence of, "Hup, two, three."

Walking without crutches I remembered the distant words, three years ago of, 'When you can walk to the door, we'll get married.' Now we were here, Paul and I facing each other over the runner, our eyes full of love and promise.

My father released me to Paul, and he took hold of my arm afraid I might fall; I'm sure I looked a little unsteady. The chapel was decorated in dewy white flowers with white satin bows, and twinkling candles stood in tall candelabra.

I had a short time to enjoy looking at the decorations because with words I was weaving my life with another. When the last vows were said, and the rings exchanged, there wasn't a dry eye to be seen.

We came down the aisle as husband and wife to the triumphant organ music and applause. Paul gave support to my left arm throughout the reception, and Max and Bob were the first in line to kiss the new bride. Now, my eyes held the tears, for each man in his generous and professional manner had helped me reach this point.

Max got the smug satisfaction that I wore his pearls. I touched them as though I knew his thoughts.

In the ensuing months, as newlyweds, we had many plans to settle. My work came to a close, Paul graduated, and we packed our household belongings and stored them in Paul's parents garage. We then traveled by car the long distance to Massachusetts to look over graduate schools for Paul. He picked M.I.T. We were lucky to find a furnished apartment on Beacon Street in Boston, and soon settled in.

One day Paul located a machine shop with the idea to custom design a pair of crutches for me. After working out the measurements and carving an arm support out of wood, he presented the ideas to the shop. Before long I had stream-lined stainless steel crutches, and the men who worked on them wouldn't take payment. The crutches were a gift to me. People can be so kind.

Many people asked about the crutches and wondered where they could get a pair, and I told them my husband had designed them. I also said the long steel rods were interest-ingly made from the gas cylinder of the M-1 rifle. With raised eyebrows they concluded I was armed in more ways than one.

Orders came for Paul to report for duty in Germany, and we just had time enough to take a honeymoon trip to Mon-tana. When we got to the great expanse, I saw a herd of elk grazing nearby in a field. Several hundred of the elegant ani-mals moved slowly about.

I squealed in delight, "Wild life!"

Paul was amused at my enthusiasm. "Wait until you see the deer come to the salt blocks at twilight."

Another first came for me when we drove to a ranch and the rancher selected a tall black gelding for me to ride. The horse eyed me with suspicion. Climbing two small steps, Paul hoisted me atop the horse. I was instructed how to hold the reins and when to use commands. Of course, that horse knew exactly how inexperienced I was and spent most of his time trying to brush me off. He kept walking under low-hang-ing tree limbs. Paul headed us out into the open fields at a walk, and my horse didn't like that either. He kept dropping his head, and I finally had to talk him out of it by pulling hard on the reins. When he obeyed my urging, he got a good patting on his mane and some words of encouragement.

After an hour of enjoying the ride, Paul decided we had gone far enough and headed us back. Once on the ground again I fed my horse a carrot and he snorted with pleasure. I patted the star on his long nose saying,"I appreciate the ride, Star, and just because I'm handicapped, I want you to know I'm no pushover."

Not once on the trip, driving out or coming back, did I see a wheelchair or anyone but myself on crutches. Where are the disabled?

It was time for Paul to depart for military service in Germany, and I could not join him for three months. I stayed with my parents, and thought my heart would break until I could join him in September.

Finally plane reservations were made, and I realized I was going to go all the way to Europe alone. I had to handle all the changes from Champaign to Chicago, Chicago to New York, and New York to Frankfurt, Germany.

Many people went out of their way to help. The day I left, I was treated like a celebrity. A newspaper photographer took my picture as I stood in the doorway of the plane, and Max surprised me by showing up at the airport to ride with me all the way to Chicago.

He surely has unlimited resources in finding out what I am doing, but I love him for it.

As we settled into our seats, Max leaned over and thoroughly kissed me with a growl low in his throat, and had the satisfaction of knowing the attendants thought he was my husband. He thoroughly unnerved me. Max took my hand in his and held it until we reached Chicago. Once arriving he saw me off on the next plane to New York. He was very serious, very much the gentleman, and very reluctant to let me go.

Once I became used to being in new surroundings, and trying out foreign languages, Paul and I found a routine to our married life. We had many marvelous encounters throughout our stay, and visited seven countries when time allowed. Nothing became too difficult a barrier, as I could take trains and buses with a helping boost up the steps from Paul.

Many people asked politely what had happened to me, and were also curious about the crutches. I still didn't see handicapped people about. Certainly not atop the Zugspitz, where I stood with my crutches in the snow looking out across the Swiss Alps, or going up and down the Eiffel Tower, or onto the water buses in Venice!

One day alone in a German department store, I bought a complete set of pure white Arzberg china. Oh, did that do my heart good. Paul thought they were quite beautiful, and went out and selected silverware to go with them.

Managing myself and a household took a lot of adapting. Crutches or my feet could slip on wet floors and scatter rugs. Carrying things like hot dishes from oven to table, running a vacuum, and picking things up from the floor required extra measures. I did the ironing, peeling vegetables or apples, and making the ends of our bed from a sitting position. I did a lot of things one-handed while hanging on to a table or counter with the other. My shoes and boots always had to have non skid soles, and my nightgowns had to be slippery nylon so I could turn myself.

Attending parties where everyone stood endlessly talking, or going to teas where everyone stood holding their steaming cups, became a trial. Someone would finally realize I was stranded and come to my aid. Paul couldn't do it all, and usually he was engrossed with the men. Sometimes people would fuss too much, and other times not enough.

The real problems to overcome were icy walkways, armless chairs, folding chairs, vans, houses with high steps, waxed floors, low commodes, deep bathtubs, and sitting too long in one position.

It took patience to figure out how to make things work.

When we returned to the States, Paul started graduate school at M.I.T., a full schedule of exciting classes with very talented students. He was really in his element. I secretly resented that his life was so well planned. That he had a base, where I seemed to be just tagging along.

Should marriage be 'the all'? I don't think so.

Then I discovered I was pregnant.

Well, that takes care of my most immediate future.

Paul became interested in what my doctor had to say, and was very careful around me. It also was a great time of waiting for our parents.

While I was on the phone to my mother one day, she told me, "Max has married. His new wife is a nationally known portrait painter. She didn't take his name, but retained her maiden name for professional reasons."

I found, to my surprise, that I was happy about that. Max was still mine in my heart.

Our wait for the baby was filled with plans for tiny clothes, furniture buying, and my getting used to ungainly weight. I was healthy, and my doctor was very reassuring. We got the surprise of our lives in my fourth month.

The doctor informed us there would be twins. Well, we had to rethink our plans. Double everything.

In the medical community of Boston about this time came exciting news concerning polio. Scientists now could see viruses with the aid of microscopes powerful enough to magnify up to visual level objects that were nearly a million times smaller than a dime. That magnification could detect clear differences in the appearances of various species of viruses. Differences from the chaotic-looking mumps virus that resembles a bowl full of spaghetti, to the absolutely symmetrical polio virus that looks as if it were a Buckminster Fuller-designed sphere composed of alternating triangles.

A vaccine was coming into being.

So, by divine inspiration I contracted an architecturally engineered virus! Paul found the whole idea interesting.

Chapter 12

❧

FAMILY DYNAMICS

Our precious sons put in their appearance near Christmas, and I became overwhelmed with motherhood and love. Paul was very proud and liked the names we had picked out, Dean and Alan. The boys were so cute I spent a lot of time just looking at them, amazed at what our love had produced.

A week later I was left alone for the first time with the new babies. I vacillated between panic and joy, but soon worked out how to bathe and feed the babies and how to organize my day. Paul figured out the logistics by putting wheels on practically everything. When the weather improved, the parents came out for a look-see, bringing gifts, news from home, and ideas to help me out.

I showed my mother the silver engraved rattles Max had sent for the boys. Dean and Alan waved them eagerly in their tiny fists. Even my sons had a tie to Max, which had been his intent.

In a year, we had toddlers, and our fenced-in yard helped keep them close by. Unlike other mothers I could not run after them if they decided to take off. Somehow they survived my clumsy learning, mostly taking the fact in stride they had a handicapped mother. Paul had also sternly instructed the boys to always obey me, or he would come home from the office and take care of it if they didn't.

I also learned that Max and his wife had produced a daughter. I sent a lovely, tiny pink dress. I loved shopping for it, longing for a daughter myself.

A year later Paul graduated and immediately set up an architectural practice in offices in Boston. He brought in a colleague from M.I.T. as a partner. Julian Andrews was urbane, witty, and a shrewd business ally. Our boys loved him, and called him Uncle Julian when he came to the house. Dean had become the pack-rat, and the tinkerer. Alan was the tidy one, and full of imagination. Julian would go to their rooms and exclaim over their toys or whatever they had to show him. He never mentioned the condition of their rooms.

As the boys entered grade school, they became very protective of me in different ways taking a cue from their father. Dean watched out for me in public, and Alan scurried after things I needed in the house. The boys were handsome like their father, they had his slim build, and the blue of his eyes. Although they had been blondes as toddlers, their hair was now becoming dark brown.

Paul and I saw to it they grew up in an environment filled with art, music, sports, and travel. This was a tall order for me to fill, and I found at times I ran on a very thin thread.

Paul was a rising star now, becoming greatly in demand, and I began to see little of him. This became one of the most difficult times for me as my stamina did not always match the demands. And I needed Paul a lot.

I joined clubs, taught Sunday school, and took over the parenting at the boys' school and their Scout troop. The boys were asked by our minister to be acolytes at the second service, and they looked very angelic in their robes with the mission of lighting candles. I only hoped they wouldn't burn the church down.

One day around three in the afternoon, I heard the boys calling for me as they came into the house from school.

They approached me in a hurry and Dean pleaded, "Mom, you have to save him. You can, can't you?"

Tears spilled down his cheeks as he held out his hand to me.

Curled in Dean's palm was a baby squirrel, fast asleep, I hoped. Alan, standing close to his brother was trying to keep his composure.

"We came down the street from school and noticed two dogs nosing the bushes and barking. We chased them away, and that's when we found the dead squirrel and the baby next to it."

"Will he live, can we keep him?" chimed in Alan. Dean was always the one to come to me to solve problems. Alan was the one who asked the most questions. Today, they were true to form.

Both boys were excited, troubled by their find, and hoping I would take over this new problem.

"I don't know, honey. He's a newborn and needs his mother." I said, appealing to their sense of right. "It seems he may have lost her though. I'll tell you what. I can call the Humane Society and see what they have to say."

Dean and Alan followed me to the phone. I looked up the number and when I reached a spokesperson and explained our dilemma, there was a short pause on the line.

"Well, first off, realistically," said the official, "The newborn has a slim chance. But if you want to take on a big responsibility, he could make it. This wild creature needs care like a real baby. And I mean around the clock."

"Tell me what is involved and how long he would be in our care," I asked, wondering if I could take this on.

There was a chuckle on the other end of the line, and I had to smile myself. This had to be other-world stuff.

"First, you will need to keep him warm in a padded box. Use a hot water bottle half filled with warm water wrapped in a towel. Try not to handle him too much, just at feedings. Then get an eye dropper, and a doll size baby bottle. He will need to be fed a formula at first with the eye dropper on a schedule."

I was writing down the directions as fast as I could, taking notice the boys were reading over my shoulder. I wrote a formula for feeding, then food such as pabulum when he started to get teeth. I thought I might be getting in over my head with the work it would take to bring the baby to an age when he could go back into the wild. But he was worth our concern.

When I hung up the phone, I could see the boys were relieved and happy that we were going to be the squirrel's new family. I hoped we would do the right things for him. Dean and Alan went in search of a shoe box, while I made a list for the market and drug store.

It wasn't long before the new boarder had a soft bed and had been named, 'Baby.' He was on a four hour feeding schedule, being fed his warm formula via an eyedropper. Each member of the family took turns. I didn't even mind getting up at night, and sometimes he hurried me with his squirrel-like squeaks. His eyes were now open, and he didn't seem afraid of his big keepers. After feedings, he would always fall asleep with a little snort when we rubbed his full rounded belly.

Paul told the whole office staff about our baby boarder, and took pictures in to show how the little squirrel looked being fed his formula.

When Baby grew a little bigger and became more hungry, he graduated to the bottle. One day after the boys returned from school, I showed them that Baby had learned a new trick. He could hold the bottle between his paws all by himself. We, as his foster family were so proud.

From then on, the little squirrel grew and grew until he needed a larger space in which to live. Paul designed a cage system with a hinged top. Inside he anchored a short tree limb, and a water dish. Baby had his blanket for sleep, and a place to scamper.

He was now on pabulum and loved it. I gave him all he wanted, and sometimes he would grab the spoon I held, or would climb into the bowl. I always kept a warm damp wash cloth nearby to clean him, and he would get very agitated and try to get away. He was starting to grow teeth and they were very sharp.

Dean and Alan told their third grade teacher about their pet, and she in turn explained to the class about the habits of squirrels. A field trip was arranged so the intrigued students could come and see for themselves. It was an interesting experience to have eighteen third-graders crowding into the house and around Baby's cage. The boys were jubilant, and Baby performed well. He chittered, climbed his tree limb, and splashed in his water bowl.

Late spring brought warm weather, and it was time to release Baby to his natural habitat. We had been instructed to take his cage outside for several hours at a time, to get Baby used to his new environment. He seemed excited to be outside, sniffed the air, and watched to see what we were doing.

Paul opened the top of the cage. Baby hopped out, ran across the yard to Dean, and ran up the pant leg of his jeans, and then perched on his shoulder. He then ran down, crossed the yard to a tall tree, and scaled the tree like he had been doing that all his life.

We laughed in unison still waiting for more antics, pleased he had become a 'real' squirrel. Finally he just disappeared, and Alan asked, "Will he get cold? Will he get lost?"

Paul answered, "No, I don't think so. He has a warm coat, and a beautiful bushy tail to keep him warm. Besides, he will be making his own nest nearby. But we will keep his cage open if he's not ready to leave. He can always come back. We will leave food for him for a few days until he finds his own."

His words satisfied everyone, but we were already missing Baby.

We saw him in the weeks and months ahead, sometimes bounding along our stone wall, and he would stop when we called his name, but he never approached. Dean and Alan had to be reminded by their father whenever they were sad about 'Baby' leaving us, that they had with their love and care given the squirrel a chance to live.

Sometimes I marveled how sensitive and kind Paul could be, those times won my heart.

Grade school, lessons in piano for Alan, guitar for Dean, and after school sports consumed the boys time. One evening Paul and I decided we needed to discuss the boys' higher education. A private school on the way to Paul's office turned out to be a good selection. He could bring them home on weekends as they would board during the week. The boys liked the idea, as the school had a great soccer team, and their art and design classes were superior.

This then started a period of discovery for me. I found out

I was entertaining myself most of the time with trivial matters, and Paul had little interest in how I spent my days. I was shocked that we were no longer involved with each other. We rarely entertained, and seldom went out. I was drifting about shopping malls without anything to do except meet friends for lunch.

God, I'm really adrift.

Engaging Paul in conversation at breakfast one morning, I asked him if he knew what I was doing with myself all day. He looked up from his paper with the strangest expression on his face.

"I'm not the sole source of your entertainment." He replied.

It was the cruelest thing he could have said to me, this was not like him. I was stunned into silence. Satisfied, he returned to his paper.

I refused to live a life of quiet and submissive desperation, and waited to see what I could come up with for activity. One day alone in the house I tripped and fell. I sat unhurt on the floor and an idea took form. I got myself up, shook off the unsteadiness and went out to do some shopping. I bought a used typewriter, paper, folders, and a metal file. When Paul came home, he unloaded the car curious about my purchases. I began to write short stories.

There was so much fun in the world, and so many ridiculous episodes to write about, I had resources everywhere. I wrote funny animal stories for the boys to read. They liked them and gave me other ideas. Little did I know a career was about to be born.

About this time Paul decided we needed a getaway, he was itching to design a summer house, and we drove to Maine to the Boothbay area. There we purchased a piece of land on which to build a house.

The land overlooked the ocean facing Christmas Cove and the Thread of Life. The Thread of Life was a treacherous channel between rocks and small islands. Birds made the rocks a haven, and I could watch them through binoculars.

It took a year to build the one-level house, from Paul's designs, and we made many trips up the Maine Turnpike to watch the progress. In April the windows were put in during a mild snow squall, as the water in front of the house churned in whitecaps.

We eventually purchased an open motorboat, and I learned to get in by sitting on the gunwale and swinging my legs over. I enjoyed trips out to nearby islands, going through inlets and harbors, and began to use descriptions of the area in my stories.

The children loved to go to our retreat, and it seemed for a while to be Paul's favorite too. Sort of an escape. Paul bought me a computer, and we would lug it with all its wires and attachments to the Maine house, along with toys and groceries. In the evenings, I would write. Paul would take the boys to play in the tidal pools a short way from the house. I think this was our happiest time.

As the boys moved into the upper grades, I immersed myself in writing a novel. Paul in the meantime became more insular, and although he was a capable and loving father, he had become an authoritative husband. He seemed to be full of criticism all the time. And since there was a lack of intimacy between us, a strained distance started to yawn.

When we were younger, I had known little of the intimacy. Oh, I had read books, but Paul was the one who had taught me. Although polio didn't hinder my ability to enjoy sex, and I didn't have trouble delivering the boys, I was now out in an arena I didn't understand.

Our relationship took a strange and polite turn.

Where had this come from?

I became very suspicious of what was going on and finally complained. We were having a quiet dinner discussing the usual subjects when I tentatively ventured into dangerous waters.

"Paul, don't you think our personal life has altered? I

don't get much affection from you anymore, and I don't know why. It makes it difficult for me to share my feelings."

Paul looked annoyed that I had brought the subject out in the open. I worried that the topic didn't warrant this kind of behavior either. We had always been able to converse about personal matters.

He placed his napkin on the table carefully folding it before answering me. His face was set, and I worried he was about to tell me something I didn't want to hear.

"You know how I am absorbed in the growth of my practice. I have to give it my total focus. Otherwise, it wouldn't succeed. You're taken care of, and the boys are doing well. Aren't they?

"I don't want to cause you any stress or discomfort. And besides, you're immersed in your own work."

"You are avoiding my question." I argued. "I'm talking about affection, and intimacy. We sleep in the same bed but are practically strangers."

I sounded like I was complaining, and I didn't even like my own voice.

Paul said, as he got up to leave the table, "You sound like a character in one of your books."

This was incredulous. He had dismissed me and my questions. My face burned in humiliation.

Have I been thrown to the wolves? A character in one of my books, how would he know? He hasn't read them.

Spending time doing research and analyzing, I put my thoughts and solutions into my first novel. The diversion helped drive way the neglect I was now feeling.

Chapter 13

❦

WHERE ARE WE?

On a torrid August morning after Paul had left for work, and it was still quite early, Max called from New York, where he was working with the National Foundation for Infantile Paralysis.

Shaking my head in awe, I thought, A straw in the wind? His timing was phenomenal.

I paused breathlessly, "It's wonderful to hear your voice."

"You're sounding pensive. Too early for me to call?" he asked as though he talked to me every day.

"No, no," I denied. "I was just sitting here thinking about the check I just received from my short story book, and just how I'm going to spend it."

Max knowingly laughed. "I have just an idea that will use some of it. Come to New York. WNYC has asked if I would agree to speak on radio with you. We will also have a panel of experts on the show, and will be discussing in an interview new medical findings about the Salk and Sabin vaccines, the handicapped, and your book. Sound good? I'll make all the arrangements. Please come."

"Oh, Max, I'd love to. When do I have to be there?"

He gave me all the particulars. I wrote them on a tablet with a shaking hand, and then we talked about our families. Neutral.

I told Paul I was going to New York to do the show.

"And I suppose Arzberg will be there?" he asked in derision.

"Yes, he will be one of the speakers," I told him. "Remember he is our friend, and a friend of my family. I see him differently than you, my life has been in his hands."

And smoothing his ruffled feathers, I added, "This will further interest in my book."

He seemed appeased as I began to make arrangements to be away for four days. I could have walked on air.

My plane arrived at the terminal, and I slowly made my way up the ramp to the open doorway. I was met immediately by a beaming Max holding pink roses in paper and fern.

He kissed me over the flowers, his eyes glittering in mirth.

"Madam Author," he announced, "I have a car downstairs to take us to your hotel."

"What a wonderful surprise to see you. I'm all yours."

"Don't I wish," he said ruefully under his breath, as he led me toward the elevators.

Outside a limousine was waiting and Max settled us inside. He placed the roses in my lap, and took hold of my hand. He couldn't take his eyes from me, and I felt scrutinized medically and personally.

I noticed Max had a few more gray hairs, and that he was fit and impeccably dressed. His gold watch gleamed in the light as he tapped our hands on his knee. He let out a long sigh.

"So, I have your every moment planned, dear heart, despite the station's schedule. I would gladly gobble up all your time, but we are professionals on call. How is Paul, by the way, and the boys? Did Paul give you permission to come? Sorry, that slipped out."

No, he was not sorry.

"Understand me, Max. I feel wonderful to be here with you. This is so special for me. The boys are great, they love their private school, and Paul is busy."

I intimated that was all I wanted to say about the family. I left him to think what he wanted, but what went through my mind as we purred along in the lovely car was, if I ever thought about an affair, I would positively have it with Max.

He hadn't changed a lot, but I had. I told him nothing of my personal life, but he knew something was different. As usual, he didn't ask.

Everything went smoothly with the network, the early schedule, and the staff. The show was informative and fun. Max and I were thoroughly on the same wavelength, as he guided our answers or encouraged me to expand on a given detail.

One rainy evening over an Italian meal at my hotel, we

reminisced about our life in the Midwest. Whereas we had taken the children to visit the grandparents each year, Max hadn't been back in years.

Max reminisced. "You know I've been traveling so much, I almost forget how big the sky is in Illinois. It stretches out a great distance, and high up as well. The weather is definitely boss. The rain doesn't tease, and the tornadoes are far from discriminating. Now out here, as I'm sure you've noticed, the sky crowds near and is more intimate. The rain does tease and the hurricanes are quick to come and go." He paused.

"Do you miss your home in Illinois? What are you thinking, I just reminded you of something?"

"No, not really. You just explain things so well I want to write them down. But what I was thinking is, I'd like to experience traveling with you and seeing things through your eyes."

Little did he know, I was longing to do so immediately.

Little did I know he caught all my inferences.

We then went up to my room for a nightcap. Max had brandy, and I had a sip or two of Amarito over ice. After talking about all sorts of things and avoiding mentioning Paul, he noticed I was stifling a yawn.

I confessed, "I'm sorry you saw that, I don't want our evening to end."

He came to my chair and leaned over, "Do you want to turn in? You've had a long, busy day."

"That's quite an invitation," I said, as I looked up into his handsome face.

"You know better. I don't tease. Now behave so that I can too," he intoned huskily. "Someone has to show some restraint."

"Yes, you're right. But will you stay a little while longer? I want to discuss what we are doing tomorrow."

Max agreed, and I rose to put on my nightgown.

"Leave the plans to me about tomorrow," he called after me. "I'll come tuck you in, and then go get some rest myself."

Max came in to sit on the side of the bed, as I pulled up the sheet. His face was inscrutible, but his eyes studied me. "You have learned more about men over the years, haven't you? I noticed a change in your demeanor at the network. You're much more self-assured."

"You're correct in that department, but you still have the most disarming smile of them all," I kidded him sinking further into the pillows.

"That's not what I meant, and you know it," he said as he picked up my hand to caress it.

"Please, I don't want to talk about the home fires," I complained frowning at him. "I'm still wounded."

"Then I guessed right, Paul has done his damage," he growled.

Max narrowed his eyes and gathered me to him in a tight embrace that had me struggling but laughing.

"I can't move, you're squeezing me too tight."

"I know, that's why I've got you pinned to my side," he grumbled feeling playful.

How I love the sounds he makes.

Max rose after he tucked the blanket under my chin. He gave me a steady gaze, pausing to let me know how difficult it was for him to leave. "Tomorrow is a discovery day," he said as he stood in the doorway. "Have pleasant dreams." And he left.

Pleasant dreams indeed! How we tempt fate knowing we can't extend our feelings, despite how delightful they are.

Ho hum.

The day dawned clear and bright. I put on an ivory slack outfit, and joined Max downstairs in the coffee shop. He saw me approaching over his newspaper, and got up to help. His aftershave smelled cool, his cheek was smooth as he kissed me. Again, his eyes spoke volumes.

Max had ordered breakfast for us, and had a car waiting when we emerged from the hotel. He did the driving and we headed out of the city to Long Island. I hugged myself in pleasure that we would have this day together alone, and Max sensed my delight by chuckling and squeezing my hand.

We had chocolate ice cream cones in a small harbor, and over the cones our eyes met in the most provocative look. It couldn't have been more sexy. We smiled at the folly of it. We continued looking around the waterways shopping for small items, and then stopped at a lovely roadside restaurant for dinner. I treasured each bite of food, every drop of wine, and all of Max's words.

All too soon it was time to return home, and Max was again taking me to the airport.

He helped me to my seat on the plane. I patted the seat next to me with a smile of invitation.

Max smiled back. "No, this time I'm not going with you, although I wish I could. None of this needs an explanation, but when next we meet, things will be very different, I promise."

He leaned down, took hold of my shoulders in a tight grip and kissed me firmly. He knew I watched him leave the plane, and I knew he watched the plane leave. We were both married, we were both testing. I savored his kiss all the way to Boston.

A month later, I received a brass plaque surrounded by a dark walnut frame for my voluntary services. Max received one too. Later I was interviewed by two newspapers in the Boston area, to again tell my story of the help I had received and its successful outcome. This was all done in response to the March of Dimes.

What affection Paul and I had for each other slowly began to wane. The boys were off at private school during the week. When they were home on busy weekends, Paul and I tried to make it as pleasant as possible. When alone, we were guarded and talked only of business, money, or arrangements for the boys.

We also were not entertaining as much or going on vacations, as Paul and Julian were flying to job sites or client meetings most of the time. But Julian managed to come to the house once every week, bringing flowers and a bag of gourmet food. He always checked on whatever I was writing, interested and adding comments. He was an excellent critic, and I valued his judgment. At least I had that.

One weekend we were invited to a dinner party that Paul could accept, and I wore a new suit that made me feel feminine and smart looking. When I appeared in the kitchen ready to leave, Paul turned from the sink setting down his glass of water. He said, "You're not wearing that are you?"

Is this a line from one of my stories?

I had momentarily forgotten how crushing Paul's criticisms could be, and still wanting to please, I pushed down my humiliation and went to put on something else. Paul made no remark when I returned a few minutes later.

Needless to say, I didn't enjoy the evening for I was still smarting. I never wore the suit again in his company, for he had ruined it for me. Later it occurred to me that I wasn't speaking up for my self enough, that I had let intimidations continue. I marshaled my forces one day at breakfast and told Paul I wasn't going to put up with intimidation any more.

"I what? When did this happen?" he asked with plain astonishment. "Anyway, you knew I was right, right? I don't know why you get so upset about what I say."

"Are you and Dad having an argument?" Dean asked, passing into the kitchen on his way to the back door.

"No, honey, just constructive discussion," I answered, hearing his doubt.

Paul kept looking at me with those beautiful eyes of his, maintaining the posture of the perfect husband with all the answers. Somehow I was living in a dream world of my own making, and needed to wake up to his flaws.

During the long spells of personal loneliness, I delved deeper and deeper into my writing. My characters began to show more depth, and I researched topics I needed. I spent a lot of time in various libraries, and always received help with my work. Books and journals were brought to me, or information was found on the computer or on film.

I ate out often, or skipped a meal when I was unduly engrossed. I kept notebooks of information, and carried a cloth tote everywhere that usually held a can of soda, a peanut butter sandwich, an apple, or a candy bar.

One day I received an agent's business card from a librarian. When I returned home, I put in a call to Maggie Conner in Boston. She told me, after our short conversation, that she would like to see a draft of my latest novel. A couple of chapters would do. I told her the manuscript had been copyrighted.

I was always in a hurry to do that; later, it was done for me.

Maggie called a week later to say she would like to meet with me, and set up an appointment with a publisher. Alone in the house, I was jubilant. I put in a call to Paul to tell him the news, but he was out. I went into the kitchen and made myself a hot fudge sundae.

My agent called two days later with a trill in her voice. The publisher had seen the work, and wanted to see us right away. Maggie was coming to pick me up. Paul was pleased when I told him what was going on with my work, and he was a little bit jealous.

The first novel to go on the market was entitled *Time Travels*. Another followed as I began to hit my stride and meet new deadlines. When the first book went into its third printing and was translated into several languages, Maggie took me out to dinner. She was a fine companion, and we shared good conversation and many laughs.

Before we started on the next book, a movie offer came from England. I was most proud of my fifth book, but the movie studio wanted to do the first novel.

Representing me was Paul's office lawyer, Bill Major. I, Bill, my agent, and editor flew to London for the interview. We studied the movie contract like we were going to war. When the contract was signed and we all went out to dinner to celebrate, I put in a call to Paul. He was amazed at the sum I was to be paid as a retainer, and mentally invested it. He also had his eyes on a building he wanted to buy for new offices.

For certain, my story would be destroyed by other script writers, I thought, but I was assured it would be intactly filmed. And it was. It was a triumph for me. It was the beginning of my thinking of myself as a professional, and that I didn't have to 'measure up.'

I knew the fur would fly after I received the first check from Bill. There would be further monies for rewrites and royalties, and Bill saw to it that everything was in my name. I invested the bulk of the amount in mutual funds after paying the legal fees.

As long as possible I put off telling Paul. Actually, six months passed while I did rewrites and stalled. Unfortunately, it all came out one night on television. Paul was watching a movie reviewer and she spilled the beans by announcing what I had been paid for the movie rights. Paul went into orbit and stormed into my office, interrupting me at the computer. His tone of voice was overbearing, meant for a child.

He sputtered, "How come I'm the last to hear how much you've been paid? I'm ashamed of you."

"Stop," I said, as I got to my feet. I needed to be on a par with him for this.

"You seem to conveniently forget that this is my career, my decision, and my money. I paid your lawyer, and the rest is in my name." My determined eyes locked with his stormy ones.

Paul wanted to get into a real argument, I could see him gearing up for one. I didn't have the energy or the emotional strength to last him out. As I moved to shut down the computer, he moved closer to me.

"I'm talking to you. Don't shut me out. There is a lot of money at stake here, and I have plans. I just hope you don't live to regret your decisions."

Turning to look steadily at him, I then left the room. I

would not be threatened. I continued down the corridor touching the side walls for balance. Entering my room, I closed the door. Softly.

Chapter 14

❦

NEW KNEE

Did all this really happen to me? Have I just been living a dream? My perfect marriage, my perfect life? No, the boys are real. Paul's office is successful. My books are everywhere. Yet, here I am again, a shell of a woman. Cared for, but not loved or cherished. Am I reduced again to being just a handicapped woman? Did I sacrifice something to get here?

On trips to Europe promoting books, I had been treated like royalty. As I traveled about I had been engaged in conversations in all languages with children and adults who had never seen a handicapped American, particularly a woman. In the cities, if I attempted to cross at an intersection, the traffic police would stop cars in all four directions, and come to escort me across the street. I got used to doors being opened before I got there, and theater aisle seats were the norm. And I was a writer, an author. *Entitled.* There was that word again. I had been given so many gifts.

I now was learning to drive a specially equipped car that had hand controls. Controls that had been designed by a paraplegic. The controls allow me to signal, change gears, wash the windows, and set the cruise control, all from the steering wheel. The suicide knob at one thirty on the wheel was the biggest hit to our two sons. They loved working on my car, keeping it purring, or driving it to games. At least I was no longer mired in the house.

Max had called off and on to fill me in on the latest advances in polio treatment, vaccines, and what they were doing about the outbreaks in Brazil. Material I needed for my books. He congratulated me on the new wheels.

"How's the driving?"

"Fabulous. I've taken some long trips, even driving up to Maine to stay at the house."

"Now you're dangerous."

"Yeah, that's exactly what someone else said."

"Oh?"

I changed the subject.

Was all this independence driving my marriage into oblivion too?

A short while later I noticed my left leg didn't hold me up as well as it should, and I took several spills that resulted in broken bones with inhibiting casts. The first bad one was near my clothes closet as I was dressing to go to a party. I started to turn and both knees collapsed. I fell and my right leg took the brunt. It started to swell immediately, and a quick ride to the hospital and the x-ray showed a broken kneecap. The disc had been snapped in two like a potato chip. That took surgery to wire the two pieces together, and six weeks of recovery in a cast.

Near Christmas, I took another fall just outside my door on a piece of ice no bigger than a quarter. Twisting when I went down, I knew I was in trouble. Somehow I managed to scoot on my fanny back into the house, grab the phone by the chord and pull it off the table. I told my doctor what had happened, and he said to stay where I was, that an ambulance would be right out. I asked him to tell the attendants not to use the siren. It screamed the entire way from town.

This time I had broken my left leg in three places.

The following day we were hosting an office party at our home for sixty people and everything was ready, including me. I greeted my guest from the sofa with a full-leg cast parked on a hassock. I wore a new long cream velvet outfit, and the boys decorated the cast with red and green stickers, and a large red satin bow on the toe. Julian acted more the host than Paul. That was one party I really enjoyed. It was our last.

Shortly after my recovery, I took another fall in the living room, but did not hurt myself. My left hand hit the floor register and dislodged the stone in my engagement ring.

An omen about my marriage?

The stone luckily didn't go down the register, and when I got back up to my feet, I put both rings in a small velvet pouch.

I visited the local jeweler later that week, and after looking over settings, selected one to hold all the stones of the wedding band and the engagement ring. When assembled, it turned out to be gorgeous. At dinner one night Paul looked at my ring and wondered why he didn't recognize it. I let him suffer.

This falling down business became a habit, and since it now seemed a little risky for me to maneuver about without added support, several methods were tried to help my weak knees. I went to Massachusetts General Hospital in Boston and was first fitted with a spoon-brace. It was molded of hard plastic and fit inside my shoe. It helped my foot clear the floor so I would not stumble.

Then we tried a series of knee braces. One doctor suggested fusing the bones of my knee and ankle, and I explained that I had already decided to never have that done.

There had been experiments with artificial knees after the hips had become a success, and I longed for one to be made that would work for me. I waited a long time for one that would give my special needs a 60 percent victory.

One finally arrived in the hands of Dr. Saint George Tucker Aufranc.

Bingo! Didn't I tell you I had an inside track?

Dr. Aufranc was tall, trim, physically strong, and had intent blue eyes sparkling with intelligence. Here we go again, with these handsome men. The architect and the surgeon got along very well, as Tucker included Paul in all the conversations about the new 'bionic' knee. Believe me, they were both very good at whatever they did, and I felt I was going to be able to have more ability than ever.

During January, I learned what the operation was about. Tucker asked many questions, studied my past medical history, and gave much thought about what he could do for me. We talked about my expectations and he assured me I would not have any more pain and that the leg would be stable.

Paul came into the examining room, and the decision was

made to have the artificial knee joint implanted. The artificial knee was made of plastic and titanium, and the whole procedure was going to be done in the most sterile conditions.

Space-age stuff.

After the surgery was complete, Tucker told me how well everything had gone, and that the new knee was a perfect fit. Actually he said, "That sucker just popped right in."

I didn't have a cast, but my left leg was hoisted up and down by a motorized pulley attached to an overhead frame. This was to keep the knee flexible. The surgical stockings I wore kept my circulation moving. Recovery was aided by Tucker's early morning visits and his wonderful sense of humor.

Also, he made some observations about how I was handling myself. I snuggled further into my bed to hear him out.

"You must admit that you have what can best be described as a challenging personality. Nonetheless, it is your personalities (the plural is intentional) that have dictated how you have handled everything so far, and they are the key.

"You have had to do what is not really possible: you were forced to change your basic personality when polio took your body apart. There was the fear and there was the pain, so you became tough. Nothing was working, so you started to question, and when the answers were less and less satisfactory, you became suspicious. With few exceptions, people were not really to be trusted. You had to be emotionally cautious, smart, focused, and above all, you had to become a survivor.

"In spite of this, I think that that side of you uses it as a tool as differentiated from your true personality: The week before you were stricken, you would have never thought about words like tough, hard, or survivor. I really believe you were and still are basically witty, somewhat cynical, determined, and emotionally soft, as in easily hurt.

"What people think of you and particularly your work really matters to you. To me this is strength. Putting yourself at risk as an author allows a distillation of what you were before polio and what you have had to become afterwards. Becoming strong when the body is irretrievably weak could not have been done alone. Amen."

He also told me, "No more freewheeling in the house. I recommend using your rolling utility cart as a walker."

I returned home to more therapy, and really missed having Bob Shelton around, but he was living in far-off Nevada. I wrote to tell him of the latest knee surgery, and he wrote back reminding me of all the things we had gone through together years ago and how happy he was for me.

Driving a car with hand-controls, managing a wheeled basket in the supermarket, and supervising the running of a household: I had received back the bigger portion of my life after all.

And the prosthesis had a warranty.

Too bad my marriage didn't.

Chapter 15

HEALING WOUNDS

Somewhere at sometime I had to transform my life. I realized my options had shut down and I needed to pick a moment when I felt strong enough to attend to them. Somehow I had been clinging to my sinking raft perpetuating sorrow long enough. This inflected misery had to be turned around. A trip up to the Maine house would do it. There I always got sorted out. My refuge.

It took three hours of driving time, with a small stop at the Dairy Queen. I couldn't hold an ice-cream cone, so I usually got one in a dish placed in a small bag with handles.

Finally reaching the house, I saw the blooming flowers I had planted in tubs were spilling over the edges, and I could hear the roar of the waves when I shut the car door. I breathed deeply of the salt air, and climbed the four steps to the walkway, lugging my carry-all over the handle of one of my crutches. The house greeted me with its peace.

The next morning, I pulled the blanket up to cover my ears, for the wind was rattling over the shingles of the roof, announcing a dark, rain-filled day. Then I reluctantly got out of bed and summoned enough energy to make myself breakfast.

Over a hot cup of tea I surveyed my kitchen cabinets for ingredients to make a pie. Before the noon whistle blew in South Bristol, I had baked an apricot pie with an almond crust. It cooled on a wire rack. The kitchen was also warm with the scent of chocolate. I had also baked double fudge brownies. I had to smile at my indulgences. Cravings had taken over my thinking about options.

All afternoon as the rain lashed the east side of the house, with gutters harmoniously gurgling, I found I had stepped out of my gloom. I rearranged the linen closet, sorting through items and stacking them in neat piles. While running a bleach wash for yellowed linens, the radio in the kitchen spat weather reports between musical interludes.

At 3:00 P.M. I made a hot cup of orange pekoe tea, realizing all the facets of my life had taken on a different appearance. I can do this; I can look outside myself, go shopping in town without just going through the motions. I can enjoy myself again. Really. I can call a friend and go out for lunch. Have a life.

Early evening and the first clearing of the storm crept through the northwest windows in slanted rays of weak sun. They spilled across the pages of a book I had started to read six months ago. Hours later I finished the book, and made preparations to go to bed. Next to the bed I kept a tablet where I jotted down ideas. I snatched it and made a list of the next day's chores, people I would call, and where I wanted to shop and for what. A sure way to dispel thoughts that go in the wrong direction.

. . .

My week away was restful and decisive. The cobwebs had been brushed away from my mind, I had new conviction, and I was ready to put my plan in action. But something new intruded. Sort of an apostrophe to my health. I noticed I was more than unusually fatigued. Pain had been creeping in gradually that required big doses of Ibuprofen. Visiting my doctor, I was surprised and alarmed that a new affliction had cropped up, called post polio syndrome (PPS).

I learned that there were six hundred thousand post polio patients, and that a great number of them were showing up at clinics and doctors' offices with complaints. The most serious complaints were pain, fatigue, and weakness. It was found that those suffering from the symptoms they had had years ago were now having them in the same damaged muscles. The worst news was that the condition was progressive. The best news was there was a lot of help.

Well, I was going to get help, fast. First it had to be established what was going on with me was really PPS. Once that was settled, I had to learn to conserve and preserve my energy. I was to do stretching exercises, take my pain relievers before the pain reached too high a level, and find a pace that worked for me for the day. Then I stopped worrying about it. It's sort of like having gray hair.

Then sad news reached me via my mother. Max had been hurriedly contacted in Europe that his wife had collapsed, and shortly after that had died. I called Max to express my sympathy, but reached his sister instead. She told me a little of the particulars, and said she would pass my message on. Denise would be staying with her while Max traveled.

I remembered the pain of extreme sorrow. One needs a place to go to be alone. I had the Maine house.

When I had been there, I had felt the tightening of the stomach muscles that worked up the chest to the throat. The working of the throat in soundless agony, the welling of tears. All that pain wanted to express itself and only sobs eased it.

So many questions, so much doubt. Did I say enough, did I do enough? I had to make peace with those demons that haunted, and soon prayer filled the void. Talking to God was so stabilizing.

Later I saw in our situation some absurdity, even folly, but we had all come out whole. The only questions that remained were, could I be satisfied with what I've been given, and be satisfied with what I have given? Is that where the balance is? I knew Max was struggling with the same questions and self-doubt. But then he had prayer too, and he would turn to it for guidance.

Oh Max, my heart is with you.

• • •

Luckily I was at home when the call came from New York.

"Ms. Jamison, I'm calling about Dr. Arzberg." My heart took a panicked leap.

"I took the liberty in calling, because I saw him reading one of your books, and I'm also a fan. He has broken his left leg in a fall on some stairs at work, and is very uncomfortable. I thought you might call or write a note to cheer him."

"Oh, you are a dear to contact me," I said with enthusiasm. "I'll do better than that. I'll come see him. Give me all the particulars, and don't mention that we had this chat."

"That will be wonderful, and I know he will be pleasantly surprised."

Explaining to Paul that I had to be in New York for a publisher's meeting (partly true), and would be gone a week, he scowled, not really wanting to loose control of my whereabouts. But I was packing, and paid no attention to his fuming.

Getting a good flight time, I arrived in New York at two in the afternoon. Plenty of time to do a little shopping for Max and get to the hospital.

When I found the private room where Max was stationed, I entered the room to find him asleep. His leg was in a cast atop several pillows. A nurse by his bed was reading a chart, and I put my finger to my lips so she wouldn't say anything. She smiled and started to leave the bedside.

Sensing a sound, Max opened his eyes, saw me, and broke into a broad grin.

"Francy, Francy," was all he could choke out.

"Poor dear, I came as soon as I heard. You can't get through this recovery alone. I'm here to help you get well." I moved toward him.

"Don't think for a moment I did this on purpose to get you here, but it worked. How long can you stay? You're wearing your hair differently, you're blonder, and I like that dress. All this for me?"

The nurse retreated from the room as I reached him. Max took hold of my arms and pulled me to his chest and kissed me. He didn't let go nor did he stop the kiss. It was lovely and passionate and stirred my inner being.

Finally I started to pull away. "Max, unhand me,"

"Oh no. Nothing makes me feel better. This is my therapy. Let me savor this, let me hold you. On a serious note, by the way, thank you for the messages of condolence. I did get them."

I stayed put, our hearts thrumming, my hands on his chest and my head on his shoulder. In his condition, the danger was moderate. He breathed in a sigh with me.

He frowned when I left his side to sit in a nearby armchair. I laughed at his consternation, and felt my fluttering heart start to settle down. Also, my cheeks returned to their normal color.

"Where are you staying, and for how long? How did you learn about my accident?" he asked all at once, as he tried to position himself more comfortably.

"I found out from your very loyal nurse. She called me at home. She's a fan of my books, by the way. I'm staying at the Carlyle for a week. I'll be here every day, so be good."

"What do you mean, be good? I'm not likely to chase you around this room. Can't I dream?" He grumbled.

I ignored his questions and pulled out of my tote bag a few magazines, a box of chocolates, a book of crossword puzzles, and a short silk blue robe. I got up and laid them in his lap.

Stepping back before he could grab me again, I said, "If you want anything else, tell me and I'll get it. But open the chocolates now. I haven't had much to eat today, and we can choose our favorites."

We spent the rest of the afternoon talking about his accident, work he was presently doing, and what book I was embarked upon. He then asked me to tell him all about my knee surgery, and Dr. Aufranc.

When I finished, he said, "I see you liked him and the way he treated you. I assume you are friends?"

"Yes, we are. I also learned to put my trust in him. For after all, I had been under his knife."

Max raised his eyebrows and reached out his hand for me. I took his in mine.

"I would have given anything to have been there with you."

The following day I had a surprise for him, and told his nurse not to let the aides serve dinner. Max looked better, a little less in pain, and was starting to get grumpy about his cast.

He watched me as I settled in my chair and took out of my tote two red apples and a paring knife. I also unwrapped a block of Longhorn cheese. Max tossed back his head and laughed until his eyes watered. I then sat on the side of his bed, peeled the apples, sliced off chunks of cheese, and fed them to him. He looked at me with pure love, and I met his gaze returning mine.

Dinner arrived shortly afterwards, catered by my hotel. It was brought in on a cart with meals for two. I had ordered Beef Wellington, small roasted potatoes, and candied carrots. Dessert was Tiramisu.

Max tucked a napkin into his pajama collar, exclaiming, "I must have died and gone to heaven."

I smiled at him in satisfaction as I cut into the fine pastry of the Wellington. "If you are really good, tomorrow you can have a glass of wine with your dinner."

"If you will have it with me, and all the days after," he said appeasingly.

"I promise you the best of my five days here."

Max had flowers in his room by now, sent by his daughter, sister, and several associates from his in-town office. Cards had arrived, and many doctors from the hospital dropped by for a short chat each day. They all took particular interest in my being there. Max loved that.

On my last day, Max was able to walk on the cast, wear his new robe, and seemed in much better spirits. He would be going home for convalescence the next day. He had help at home, and a lot of research to do on the computer and the Internet; the world was calling for his fine ideas. His work would help make his recovery go faster.

We had a long, drawn-out goodbye. Steadying himself near the door, we made polite conversation.

"Aren't we a pair? Both of us on crutches. I'm sure you could beat me in a race down the hall. I'll never forget your first steps. You were so disgusted, you wanted more."

He then cupped my face with tensed fingers, kissed me, made a firm promise, and let me go.

The flight out was uneventful, but I did request a glass of wine as I thought about what Max had said. I grinned in remembrance.

'Next time I will have two feet, watch out.'

Keep teasing me, Max, I want to believe.

Chapter 16

❦

BROKEN PROMISES

Returning to Boston was emotionally hard, but I had accomplished what I had gone to New York to do. Max knew it was a sort of pay-back, but more a reestablishing of a sound friendship. All of it had endured, and a lot more. My publisher was also satisfied with our short meeting in his office.

Another trip up to the Maine house found me on the deck enjoying the warm sunny day. The sky was a canopy of cloudless blue blending to pale yellow on a sharp water horizon. The wind out of the southwest pushed an outgoing tide into building combers that stretched their waves clear across the bay. People piloted their boats over the spilling foam hurrying back for 'happy hour' on their own decks.

One boat passed closed by and the owner seeing my stars and stripes fluttering, sounded his horn in greeting. It was our marina owner, and I waved to him.

Such was the passing parade in my life at that moment. I had been writing in long hand for several hours, and decided to go in and transfer the material onto my lap-top computer. I was 200 pages into a new novel that was progressing at a good speed, and I didn't want to loose the pace or connections.

As I entered the house through the sliding doors, the phone rang. I knew who it was before I answered, because it was Friday, and Paul was due here in three hours.

Paul was exuberant in speech as I answered the phone.

"Hi, it's me. You won't believe who I just heard from. Our proposal for the plaza project was accepted, we have the go-ahead. Isn't that great?"

He didn't wait for my answer but hurried on.

"This is a huge project and we were selected over five other architectural firms. It's good we're nearly through with the library project, because we'll need the entire staff for this one."

"Good for you," I said, "It was a good plan and I think you deserved it. Plus you were saving the client money."

"Well, needless to say, with all the excitement, I'll not be coming up this weekend. Sorry, but you do realize we're up to our necks now. The boys were disappointed when I called them, but they understood. They said to tell you if they can get a ride they will come up."

When we ended our conversation, I wondered why I ever bothered to second guess him.

. . .

After I came back from my Maine trip, Paul phoned from the office one afternoon to suggest dinner out. Things had been cool and polite between us for a long time, and I concluded he was making an effort to move our relationship into warmer waters. Why, I didn't know.

"Could you bring my other briefcase with you, the black one?" he asked. "It holds some papers I need."

I glanced at the calendar on the refrigerator, noting the boys weren't due back from their kayaking trip for four days, and told Paul I'd be at the office at five.

Paul, with his usual one-track mind rambled on. "Julian and I are still in the midst of the university scheme, and we'll be charetting for days. We've hired an extra staff of draftspersons just for this project, and the computers are humming."

With my life, and my love life, still hanging suspended, I wondered what this dinner would produce. I decided to take a leisurely bath and proceeded to the master suite. I poured bath salts in the tub and sank into the hot water, thinking about the long hours Paul's team was putting in. They were all dedicated and loyal, and we were fortunate to have them. This was a stressful time, and I was glad Paul decided to take a break and go out to dinner.

After a long soak, I reluctantly worked my way out of the tub and toweled dry. I dressed in an apricot colored suit with a cream and apricot checked blouse, and put on the diamond earrings Paul had given me on our fifteenth wedding anniversary. This was only the second time I had worn them. I took one last look in the mirror at myself, saw the doubt in my eyes, but nodded in satisfaction. I went in search of the keys.

Driving into town was always a thrill on a good day such as this. I hummed to myself as I thoroughly enjoyed the sun bouncing off the tall buildings, glinting in the high windows. The skyscrapers made a dramatic backdrop against the azure sky. Boston has such vitality.

Arriving at the parking garage to Paul's office building, I parked in a space near the elevators and the stronger lights. Entering the elevator, I rose quietly up to the twenty-first floor. When I went through the doors of our offices, I found everyone in an efficient frenzy. As usual, there were dozens of deadlines to meet.

I greeted the secretaries, Marge and Janet, who paused for a moment from their keyboards to return my greeting and have a short chat. Marge then told me the men were in the conference room, and I left to stroll down a long corridor that opened to other rooms.

I looked into Paul's office and found it empty. His desk was cluttered with papers. I stood and looked around admiring my decorating. Beside the large desk near the windows were all sorts of electronic devices and a complicated phone system. On the other side I had created a seating area for consultation that spoke of elegance and confidence. I had movers place two maroon leather chairs with side tables beneath a grouping of four watercolors. I had selected hunting scene table lamps and a heavy mahogany coffee table. Paul never did know what the custom-made rug and drapes had cost.

I studied the gate-leg table with the silver coffee service that sat against one wall. I had found both in an antique shop. Both had been used a lot, and had a fine patina. I had done this a long time ago just after the boys had been born. Paul had cautioned about the strain of coming into town so often. I laughed that the babies were destined to be architects anyway.

The office had changed little since new paint, another state-of-the-art phone system, and a different director's chair had been installed. Paul had wanted one like Julian's. He found a duplicate in an antique's store. The office had a feeling of peace that stood in contrast to the hectic affairs that were conducted here.

I walked over to the long, high windows and looked down at the park below. I had always loved this view. I thought about Julian for a moment, what a solid person he was, and how we enjoyed his company as well as having him for a partner. He never married, seemed to have several women on the string for a while, but preferred sports and his hobbies. He was competent at whatever he pursued. Where Paul was dark-haired with intense blue eyes, Julian was sandy-haired with soft gray eyes. Paul was slow to humor, and Julian was full of spontaneity.

Enough of this wool-gathering. I turned and went in search of the two men.

Soundlessly nearing the conference room I heard noises of rustling papers, then a quiet that seemed to close in the room. My first image was of the mirrors on one wall that rose from floor to ceiling. Reflected there was a scene that paralyzed me with shock. My eyes registered the truth, but my mind failed me. Their embrace was not an accident, it was intimate.

Shattered and confused, I turned and managed to get down the corridor and out the doors without causing attention. An elevator arrived to take me to the parking level. Feeling with instinct only, I got the car in gear and headed for the turnpike. I noticed that no one had followed.

Driving home was a nightmare. My tumbling thoughts warred with the rapid traffic. I steeled myself to keep my wits, and got home safely. I had to push back thoughts and vowed not to break down. Arriving in my own driveway, I sat in the car choking back sobs.

Oh yes, there had been signs I had ignored, I reminded myself as I went over a litany of events. I'll have to sort this out. They will expect me to, and want my love and acceptance. How many of our friends know? Tears spotting my blouse, I realized the boys would have to be told.

I wearily entered the house and started another bath. One to wash away the sins of my husband, and howl in anguish as the betrayed woman. After giving in to the mindless sounds, I stilled them with a wash cloth over my mouth. Somehow that calmed me, and I reasoned I had to salvage something from this, and that would be my strength. I couldn't give in to total despair, I had learned that from Max. Anger took over instead.

I put my long, rose-colored robe on over a nightgown, and went to the kitchen to make something to eat. Finding I could only eat toast, I made mint tea to go with it. When I looked around at the lovely kitchen that Paul had designed, I found I now hated it and him. My feelings for him had banked a long time ago, and what had been goals and fun had diminished to boredom. But I had never given up hope. Now, hope was a memory.

Chapter 17

TRAVELING SOLO

As I finished my second piece of toast, I saw car head-lights swing into the driveway and knew the moment of truth was at hand. I heard Paul's car stop, and heard footsteps on the gravel walk. Thank God the boys weren't here. This confrontation was only between us. I got up and walked to the counter. Better to be on one's feet. I would not be intimidated.

Paul came into the kitchen from the porch, with his car keys jingling in his hand. I used to love that sound. As the light illuminated his face I could see the strain, guilt, and wariness. I wasn't sorry for him at all.

He stood just inside the door, not knowing whether to come all the way in or not.

Clearing his throat, he shook his keys in a nervous gesture, and said almost in a whisper, "They told me you had left. I was not sure what to do first, so I came here. I know you didn't know, but I had every intention of telling you when the time was right."

He cleared his throat. I took a deep breath almost ready to explode, but knew I wouldn't gain any ground with loss of control.

"Well, it's now," I said with some sarcasm, looking at my one-time husband. "You waited just a bit too long and now the damage is done. Congratulations."

I returned to my chair and suggested that he should sit. He slumped into one. I studied this man I had been married to for over twenty years, the devoted father of our two children and the one I had vowed to trust and give my fidelity to. Had it all come down to these final words?

At that moment a very clear picture emerged that warned me. Although my love had been traded for another, and a betrayal stretched between us like an unforgiving barrier, I possessed new control and had better use it carefully.

With more calm than I felt, I asked, "I'm having mint tea. Do you want some, or do you want a drink?"

He got up and came back to the table with a cup, no saucer. I poured, my hand steady.

"I'm a lot more composed now than when I got home," I said with measured tones. "I've had my hysteria and rage. It would be useless to attack you. You made your choice a long time ago."

His eyebrows went up at that remark. "So, you have had doubts before?"

"Yes, and how like strangers we have become, so polite. The gulf between us is much wider now," I said reproachfully. I narrowed my eyes as I looked at him, and wiped away a small drop of tea from the table.

"I need a full week to sort things out," I said. "Why don't you pack clothes you will need, and stay in a hotel near work? With this charette going on, it will be most convenient."

I had given him an out. He took it.

"What are you going to do? Nothing rash I hope?" Paul asked, knowing things were over between us and guessing he still had some advantage.

"Not much. Think, decide where I go from here," I answered with a long sigh.

Paul had always been a man of few words, but he looked like he had a lot on his mind as he struggled with the emotional toll.

"We have serious plans to make. I can't deal with it now with all this work facing me. I promised that I would take care of you, and I will. You don't have to worry about that."

Well, thanks Paul, now you're off the hook.

Bitterness was choking me, and I tried to push it aside as he rose from the table and proceeded through the house to his closet.

When Paul left, his shoulders slumped as though the burden was only his. I felt like I'd been hit by a cyclone, and had been left shattered and wounded. My face smarted, and I was torn in two. I took a sleeping pill that night. It worked.

The next day, although I looked like a wreck, I knew I had to get organized. I moved slower than usual, almost afraid to step on the broken shells of my marriage. My computer was dark and waiting, representing wonderful stories full of hope and love, things I couldn't face.

I sat in an armchair drinking a cup of orange-flavored tea, looking out the dining room window watching the birds, for I felt lost and adrift. Why has God abandoned me? Why am I forsaken? Why am I always losing things?

A cardinal flew by the windows, his scarlet flame a blur, and I saw life moves on. Could I move with it? Thoughts intruded of what I had, and I wondered if I could make something positive out of all of this. Paul's remarks last night reminded me of our parents, and their reaction to this turn in events. I didn't think I could draw them into our affairs at this time, it was too soon. Paul and I needed to trim our explanations. This has to be terminal embarrassment for us, and what an ending!

Max had once said, "When one door closes, another one opens."

God, are you listening?

It took three days for me to finally shake myself free of the emotional trial. I had let myself mourn. I called a realtor. Making an appointment for her to see the house, I asked about houses for sale in the Cambridge area. She suggested Newton. Then I marked a large calendar with a black pen the dates when I wanted things to be settled, adding phone numbers of people I had to call. I couldn't continue with my latest book until this marital dust settled.

The boys returned later in the day from their trip with exciting stories to tell me, and I half listened, worrying how I was going to explain this latest development. Since Dean withholds his deeper emotions, and Alan lets them out, I knew firsthand that I couldn't handle explanations at this time. With new resolve, I decided Paul could take that on.

Thank you, Lord. Now we're clicking!

When the weekend was over, I called Paul to set a meeting date for Friday noon in his office. I had made many decisions. I told him to have Julian present. He agreed, somewhat hurried, but respectful.

Friday came, and again I rose in the elevator with an entirely different feeling: emotionally fragile, but determined, and a little bit nervous. I greeted the secretaries, and proceeded to Paul's office. The men were waiting for me. Julian, suave and pensive-looking, came forward to kiss me on the cheek. Paul remained standing, all hard-edged, near the desk until I was seated. I laid my crutches on the floor next to my chair.

I had spent a lot of time on my appearance. I had had a facial, makeup, and nails done, and had bought an expensive suit that was not only attractive but fit like it was made for me, and did wonderful things to my eyes and hair. I had brought in with me a new slim briefcase that held pages outlining our future.

I pulled from the valise three folders, one for each of us. Julian opened his immediately and glanced at the typed pages. Paul tapped his unopened one with suspicion.

"What's this, an ultimatum? You know I won't stand for that. What claims you have must be okayed legally."

Julian touched his hand in warning, and Paul snatched it away with a scowl.

I would not have my feelings ruffled and proceeded.

"If you both will read the first page, you will see I've worked out a few things that could turn out well for all of us. But everyone here at the table has to agree. None of us wants an unsatisfactory conclusion."

Both men studied the first page. I saw Julian nod, and then smile. Paul still had a dark look, but was softening.

"I looked at the duplex this morning in Newton. It's about a twenty-minute drive from here. But, the most important fact of a move for all of us is the boys need access to their father."

Paul looked relieved. I hadn't gone wild, I had been rational. But I knew he was still apprehensive. I continued.

"The duplex is new, has plenty of driveway space for cars, and a huge backyard. Julian, you can have a garden there. You'd like that, I know."

I looked at him and saw the dawning pleasure on his face.

"Paul, the first page covers living arrangements, and the realtor for our house has suggested a very handsome price, as you can see. It more than covers the cost of the duplex."

"On page 2, if you will turn to that, I have outlined what terms I have worked out."

"Oh here it comes, the demands," Paul said without looking at the page, and of course trying to make me out as the villain. I had been there before

"There are three terms. I would like sole ownership of the house in Maine. I will live in the duplex, pay my own bills, if we agree, for three years. The boys will be through college then. At the end of that time, I want a final legal separation with no financial exchanges."

I had expected Paul to be in shock, but he wasn't. Cool as ever in a crisis, he looked at me with speculation. Julian was eager to agree to it all.

Finally Paul shifted in his chair and said, "If, and I stress if, we decide on these plans, I want it all in writing. A copy for each. I want Bill to go over these terms."

I didn't know whether I wanted to shake his hand or slap him. He had used me in an unforgiving way, and this was how I was treated. Julian wanted to smooth the emotional upheaval, and cautioned Paul that the ideas were sound and would work for all of us. That it was a brilliant plan, fair, and generous on my part. Paul eventually backed down. I could see him mentally shift.

Oh, he didn't want to admit I was right.

Giving Julian a grateful nod, I noticed the caterer came in with our lunch. Julian had selected a splendid luncheon, but I couldn't eat a thing. I selected lemon tea, and had trouble swallowing even it.

Over his plate, Paul decided we had a deal. It was workable. I was too excited to take it all in just then. But it was decided, I would sell the house and organize our furniture. Paul would see to the duplex, and what was needed like connecting doors and ramps for me. Julian would contact movers for his things and ours, and plan the garden and landscaping.

It was amazing to me how quickly we could completely transform our lives. It was as though it had been there waiting. When I rose to leave, I had one parting shot for Paul. I instructed him to collect the boys, take them to dinner, and tell them of the move. I think he hated me a little at that moment.

I received small satisfaction from my visit to the office, but I had done all I could to make a peaceful transition. Considering what had transpired, I had been forced into this position.

As I drove home I passed a lovely restaurant that was still serving lunch, backtracked, and found my way in. I ordered wine and a shrimp salad. This survival course had made me hungry after all.

Chapter 18

❦

RENEWED TREASURES

When my book, *The Celestial Committee* came out, I appeared at a book signing in New York City. The signing started at one o'clock and really went well, especially with my agent and editor seated next to me.

I looked up as the next book was opened before me, and gave a small shriek of delight. To the surprise and interest of all those in the store, I rose from my chair, and edged around the table into Max's arms. He laughed as he held me. A quick kiss, and he helped me to return to my chair.

"I will see you when this is over. I'm taking you to dinner," he told me in a whisper.

I didn't want to let go of his hand, and beamed with radiance that had nothing to do with signing books. But I signed his book so he could leave. I watched him all the way out of the store.

His book had a special message, 'All my unrestrained love, Francy Holland.'

Several hours later, we were together in Max's suite, sitting on the sofa going over the day's events, and where we had left off from our last time together.

I learned he had tracked my latest book, found out when I would be in, and had stationed himself at the coffee center in the bookstore to wait for me.

"You see, Max, no matter how I may sometimes deny it," I said with a rueful smile, "*The Celestial Committee* brought us together."

Max leaned toward me, "Despite what you just said, the thing I noticed about you that occasionally came up was your willingness to face difficult situations. You just dove in with a determination that bordered on supreme heroics. I couldn't figure it out at first, but then it came to me one day that you weren't just coping, you were calling on all your various resources, things outside yourself for complete and fair solutions. That 'committee' had to have been one of them."

I sat on the brocaded sofa, gathering resolve to tell him what I had wanted to tell him for years. In fact I had told him most of it in my dreams. Now he was sitting here holding my hands studying me.

Max said with all earnest, "You're more composed, more mature with your success."

How dear a man he is, how lucky I am to have been found by him. I'll probably write about this episode one day, it would make a wonderful love story.

I wanted to take a sip of my cool wine, but didn't want to remove my hands from his, so took a shaky breath and started to explain.

"As I glance back over the progression of events, I see times of agonizing decisions. The antitheses were the overwhelming successes, sound choices, and team efforts worked out between Paul and me. Paul knew my weaknesses, physically and emotionally, and knew where to give support."

Max looked doubtful.

"I once wanted desperately to hide in a shadow, for I felt so vulnerable. Then I found refuge in my husband's shadow. Later, I had to form a different attitude and emerged to cast my own.

"Through the most difficult years, I found out the minute I thought everything was the way I wanted it, I only had to turn a corner to see it fall apart.

"Once inside a disaster, I was in for the duration. That duration led me down untried paths into detours I would never have chosen. A straight line did not always take me where I needed to go. The people who took me on the various life-journeys made a major impact, a positive one, and they never gave up on me. Just like you. Your generosity of heart and spirit impelled me to stretch both mind and body.

"You remember I am talking about a teenager, then a young woman, whose life's quality had been reduced physically and emotionally. Although my spirit was tested time and again, it took all my physical energy to wage the war that would give me the victory I wanted. You remember, dear Max, you were there throughout that siege.

"Then a door opened for me and the skill of writing made itself known. I was off and running, running on a computer. I started writing books, poetry, short stories, novels, and anything that desired to be written. It seems I had a backlog, a logjam of stories I wanted to write. They were piled up waiting, and they had things to say, many times about the handicapped.

"Through all the years I traveled back and forth to Europe, one stark and phenomenal truth stood out: There weren't any disabled persons around. They were not on planes, trains, beaches, or in churches, theaters, or museums where I went. Thousands and thousands of them were invisible except for me.

"Then motorized carts and wheelchairs were developed and the physically challenged began to appear. They got organized and began to talk to architects and politicians about having access to public buildings and transportation. They were not going to wait to be saved, they were taking action. I had a great sense of pride when Paul began designing projects with access ramps for buildings and train stations, for he knew firsthand what was needed."

Max nodded, letting me spill out the philosophical results of my thinking.

"Over the long haul, it did take a long time for me to settle down with a humorous and patient menu. Thank God, I had reachable dreams. Throughout all this time we have been apart, Max, during times of great stress, I called out my tools. You taught me that. You showed me where the fight was, and supported my learning how to use my mind in the battle."

Max was following every word and wouldn't interrupt.

"You can't know how lonely it all was, all this time, but it taught me to be observant to nuances in others' behavior. I absorbed details and didn't know how much private information I had caught. What I mean to say is, I picked up things I wasn't meant to know. All of it culminated in writing some of

it down as therapy. I was amazed that it sounded so interesting and began to develop some of the themes into stories.
The stories went into novels and there you have it. God, did I
say all that? Have I worn your ear off?"

Max smiled, shaking his head 'no.' He didn't release my
hands the entire time I spoke, for he was thinking—

—I feel tremors running through her body to my hands. I
am heartened to hear her let go of this burden, and especially
elated that she feels like confiding. Maybe I can make some
headway. But I won't rush, nor make a fatal maneuver and
loose her. Sometime later I will tell her what had been on my
mind a long time ago in Champaign, but only after I know I
have won her heart.

I didn't guess I had picked up on his thinking and felt a little mischievous. "This is probably a dangerous question, but
I'm going to ask it anyway. It's one I've been wondering about
for a long time."

"Go ahead, you will no doubt use my answer in one of
your novels."

"Ah, not exactly," I said a little out of breath. "Years ago
in your apartment when you gave me the lovely pearls, were
you trying to seduce me?"

Max let his eyes smile while he pursed his lips delaying
his answer.

"Yes, I was," he finally admitted.

"Well, my real question is, why didn't you?"

He passed his hand over his face trying to wipe away a
grin.

"You really want to know, don't you? All right, I'll give you
the truth. I was seven years older, and wanted to settle down.
You were on the brink of discovering a new life. Much to my
regret I didn't just sweep you off your feet and rush you into
accepting me. I know if I had kissed you, you would have surrendered. I'm correct aren't I?"

He didn't wait for my answer, but pulled me into an
embrace.

"Star struck, that's what we were." His fingers traveled my backbone in little familiarizing strokes. His body felt solid as we studied each others faces marveling how we could be this intimate and unguarded.

Alas, we had to part and resume reserved postures.

We chatted for a good hour, and then Max suggested a trip the next day to Connecticut to see his home.

Time was repeating itself.

I told him after a noon signing at the bookstore, I was free. He could pick me up at my hotel at two. And I didn't feel guilty, regretful, or apprehensive.

Chapter 19

❦

SAFE BUT SORRY

The next day, after a good night's sleep, Max arrived at my hotel in his car.

"How can we ever catch up with each other?" I asked as we moved through the traffic and made the turn onto the long parkway.

His hands steady on the wheel, Max gave me a quick glance. "Do you think we need to? We have a lot of time ahead? Let's take it a day at a time. You say you have three days? You're my guest, and I have a first-floor guest suite that will suit you just fine. We can discuss important matters, like our children, my trip to Europe, and your obligations to your publisher. Our careers have evolved, and I want to know where you are headed. But first, I want to speak about our feelings and what has survived."

I agreed with him, but my heart started doing flip-flops every time I looked at him.

"Max, my dearest dear, a lot has survived, otherwise we wouldn't be here so excited like two teenagers in love."

I touched the sleeve of his jacket and he covered my hand capturing it in a firm clasp. I took another deep breath and realized I would be doing that a lot with him, as he filled me with powerful emotions.

The drive was smooth for some distance and car lights were beginning to come on when Max suggested we stop for dinner at a little out-of-the-way shack he knew along the coast.

Giving him a doubtful look, I asked, "A shack? You? We'll just see about that, but I'll bet they have clam chowder."

Max smiled a secretive grin and turned the wheel to take the off-ramp. After a few miles we pulled into a parking lot in front of a weathered low building that indeed looked like a shack. It was tied into a Marina and tall sailboat masts could be seen rising behind it.

Max helped me get out of the car, gave me the crutches and steered us toward the restaurant with a hand at my elbow. Once inside, we were met with delectable aromas of cooking herbs. A tall wooden hutch to our right held casserole platters on each shelf filled with bread pudding, apple crunch, and peach cobbler. Small candles winked from glass jars placed strategically among the platters, and bright blue pottery plates stood straight like soldiers along the back.

Feeling welcomed by the scene of scrumptious food, we admired original oil paintings on the walls as we were led to our table.

I was pleased to see a single pink rose in a vase at the center of the white tablecloth, and place settings of blue china with blue water goblets. The charm and the nice touches were a pleasure.

After being seated and reading the short menu, we placed our orders. When the wine was poured, Max took my hand in his, interlaces our fingers, and proposed a toast. "To us."

He pondered, Can she love me? Am I right to steal her away like this?

I noticed his preoccupation, and released my hand to sit back and contemplate his face. "Whatever you are silently asking yourself, my answer is, yes. But let's savor this time together. I know from experience, as you do, and all the characters in my books know, that something could come along and mar it. That I couldn't bear."

"Not this time," he vowed over the rim of his glass.

Steaming chowder and fresh-made bread were set before us, momentarily interrupting our train of thought. We eagerly dove into our meal, covertly watching each other.

Conversation now centered around the work Max was doing and his travels. He would soon be going to Rio de Janeiro, Brazil, to get reports on the epidemics of polio that were showing up in the northern states. Unlike the United States, an immunization program had not been started there. He was going to suggest such a program. I was thrilled for him, and fascinated with the scope of his influence.

Over peach cobbler and coffee Max probed, "Do you feel like talking about Paul?"

I was embarrassed my marriage had taken the turn it had, but I was going to tell him anyway. I put down my spoon and leaned toward him in confidence. "All the events were so unexpected after Julian, but you will understand when I tell you a few things."

"What's this, Julian, Paul's partner?" Max asked with trepidation.

"No, wait, don't jump to conclusions. There is something you need to know first. Let me back up and establish a setting."

And I began. "It was a beautiful day. Paul called me at noon and suggested dinner in the city. I was to meet him at the office at five o'clock. I drove in wearing a new suit and the diamond earrings he had given me for our fifteenth anniversary.

"I reveled in the beauty of the city skyscrapers piercing the blue sky as I rolled along the turnpike. I thought how fortunate I was to have such a full life, even if Paul and I were at odds. Arriving in the underground parking lot, I was ready for the unexpected evening out.

"I left Paul's briefcase on his secretary's desk, and she told me the men were in the library conference room. I assumed they were concluding a meeting. At the double doors that were slightly ajar, I could look into the room. There were long mirrors flanking walls of paintings and book shelves, and in one I saw something that didn't quite make sense at first. "When I identified the two men, I turned with a gasp and left the offices in shock. I don't know how I got home, but I did. The men, their looks and touches, washed over me, and my marriage, as I saw it, was over."

I lowered my head, not saying or seeing anything.

Max almost rose from his chair, remembered he was in a restaurant, and grabbed my hands instead, shaking the thin vase, "You mean Paul and Julian, they were lovers? My God, Francy!"

His concern wearied his face, and he pounded our hands softly on the table for emphasis.

I leaned forward and placed a finger over his lips, stilling the outburst, struggling to find the words to assure him.

Haltingly I answered, "Yes, they are, but in the best of ways I later learned. They are so good as partners, Max, so super with the children and me. The legacy is, I gradually came to grips with it."

My expression became more earnest and almost bitter. "I wanted to call you the instant I knew, and explain that you were right. Pour it all out, win your sympathy, say he was wrong for me and why. But I knew I had to live it through. Live out my obligation. I think we are all better for it, my moment of clear unselfish decision, my emotional investment."

"I would have come to you, I would have helped in any way I could," he growled, angry with the fate of it. The lost time was the worst, and the arrogance of Paul who had to have it all.

Over the flickering candle, my eyes met his. "Don't be a doctor now. I don't want to be your patient. Console me. Accept this situation. Be my love. That is what I want now."

The atmosphere seemed to change abruptly in the whole restaurant. Max placed his napkin on the table and rose from his chair.

I started to laugh and held up my hand. "No, no, not now, you clown."

"Why not?" he asked as he reached my chair. "No time like the present, I've waited a long time to hear you say that."

He brushed my hair away from my face with his hand and lightly kissed my temple.

I took a long breath and sighed, and he whispered, "That's what I like to hear. Let's go to the car before I do something else that will shock these innocent patrons."

Leaving the restaurant after Max paid our bill, and not being able to control myself, I giggled all the way across the parking lot. The vision of the elegant Max making a faux pax in public was too much. Once inside the quiet and dim interior of the car, Max turned in his seat and slowly gathered me to him. He kissed me until I had to push away for air.

"Max, you're stealing all my breath. I don't want to fight you."

He grinned a wicked grin, and then growled deep in his throat. I shivered and let him do what he wanted.

I don't need air, I need this spiraling into oblivion.

Max promised himself, I'll not let go of her this time.

It was dark and late when the car's wheels ground into a gravel driveway, and we arrived at his home. Max touched a remote control switch in his hand and lights sprang on around the house and walkway. Once inside Max took me on the grand tour, and then got us settled in the living room. He turned lamps on low, and I felt cozy and comfortable. I leaned back into the cushions of the sofa, stretched out and tucked my feet under a pillow.

"Tell me about our early days. I want your perspective," I began as Max settled near me. He laced his fingers together over his chest. His look was reflective, and he was remembering with great pleasure.

"Our story started during a polio siege in Champaign, Illinois. I was given the position of setting up and overseeing a new isolation hospital and all its future patients. One day at the end of summer, a defiant young woman came in as an unsuspecting polio patient, and she touched my heart. I didn't know its ramifications for some time.

"I couldn't do too much for her medically as the disease devastated her body. All I could do was see that she had lots of liquids and pain medication. She went in and out of one crisis after another. At one time we thought we were going to lose her.

"The outcome was, I became more involved than was prudent, and we ended up having one of those chaste, frustrating relationships. Over those years you were nearly the death of me, Francy."

He looked at me with penetrating eyes that couldn't have been darker. I bit my lower lip, remembering.

He continued with a serious expression. "I only wanted you to be happy, and you seemed to have found your happiness. But I had a hard time accepting your decision."

I covered my face with both hands, trying to shake off the mental picture of how he had been hurt.

He pulled down my hands, "You didn't want to admit it, but you knew I loved you. You parried nicely. You chose that boy not knowing he had flaws and one focus only, his career. He was possessive of you and you responded in your need. I could do nothing to counter it."

I interrupted. "I know that now. Do you remember my book, *Time Travels?*

"Yes," he admitted, "I saw through your characters and knew that you had arrived at the same conclusion. All your books directed me where you were going in your thinking. I always felt close to you."

"Then you know much more about me than I do of you. It was always that way wasn't it?"

"We'll rectify that shortly," he promised me. "When you left for Europe, I stayed in Chicago for a symposium sponsored by the National Foundation for Infantile Paralysis. That's where I met Connie. She was already a known portrait artist with a stunning career, and she attended the meeting with another doctor. She was a very upbeat lady and we started seeing each other. We married a year later and eventually along came Denise, our only child. We called her De De. She is lovely like her mother was, and is now an illustration artist for Vogue magazine. She lives in Chicago and is twenty-two.

"That was the age I lost you."

I closed my eyes and sighed. "Did you ever tell your wife about the events in Champaign?"I asked self-consciously, wanting to slide over the agony of his last words.

"Oh, yes, she heard the whole nine yards. And, by the way, she collected your books and loved them. She thought it was sweet we knew each other."

"My involvement with the Foundation led to the March of Dimes Committee, and then the World Health Organization. There I finally took a leadership role. I bought a house in Connecticut. Connie had to commute most of the time from Washington, D.C, while De De was in school. But we made the best of the separations, managed some lovely times together.

"I was in India when Connie was stricken. She was in Washington, working on a commissioned piece, a wonderful oil, when she collapsed. It was a major stroke. I quickly returned, but no matter what was done for her, or who I called for help, she never got better. Denise and I sat by her bed, willing her to recover, but as it turned out we only had time to settle her affairs. I loved my wife, and I loved her the day she died. She never knew what I felt for you, any more than abiding affection."

He looked at me with the most intensive expression, and I waited for his next words. "But it was a love I realized I had put on hold."

Max sighed deeply and resumed in a lighter tone. "But what I want to know is, when did you start to write, and what triggered it?"

I smiled ruefully, shaking my head. "It started after I fell down."

Max frowned and appeared worried.

"No, I didn't hurt myself. It was all pretty foolish. I sat on the floor at home, in the first house, thinking I couldn't have my dreams, any of them. Whenever I was in a down mood, I seened to dwell on things I had lost as though that was my fate.

"That's when it occurred to me that I could have my dreams. Lots of them. I could pull together all those short stories and ideas I had tucked away in a file, and drag them out and write books.

"When I got started, I drew upon experiences. You would show up in those pages. I liked that, but sometimes it was very painful. I knew my marriage was a farce, but didn't know why or what to do with it."

Uncontrollable emotions spilled over, and I wiped away warm tears. "You know, Max, I once wanted to crawl into your lap, have you hold me, and shut out the world. Selfish, I know. That was in one of the hospitals. Later, I wanted much more. But by then it was too late. By then fair and right were just words."

Max pulled the pillow from my feet, carefully removed my sandals and placed them side by side near his feet. He then scooped up my legs and placed them across his own. He circled his arm around my waist and drew me closer to his left hip.

"There you are, just where you wanted to be. We're not talking fair, we're talking fulfilling dreams. Yours and mine. I only hope it won't take too long to get there."

Resting my forehead against his chin, I smiled at his words. He placed a hand under my chin and lifted my face. I closed my eyes, giving myself up to his kiss. We were both startled by the quick passion it evoked, wanted it, and continued deepening our intent. We each knew in those minutes we were bonding a found love.

Breathless, we drew apart, and regarded each other. Our eyes brimming with discovery and sadness.

The dance of flirtation, revealing nothing, promising something. The thrill of discovery, the warmth of recognition. We take two steps forward, then one step back, we provoke, parry, and demure. Who will be the winner, who the aggressor? Who will give in, who will give most? Where is this going? Where do I want it to go?

On the other hand, if I don't let this move forward, I've lost the chance of learning about the 'what ifs.' Is it worth it? God, Yes.

My boys are in school forty miles away. I am still married, and he is a widower.

When Max drove me to Boston three days later, as he insisted, we were still savoring our time together. We had had a wonderful time exploring harbors on his boat, eating out or eating in. We had even gone to a movie, had pizza afterwards, and strolled some late opened art galleries.

When we arrived at my home, Max grew quiet and looked around the duplex with unconcealed anger. He drew me into his arms and gave me a fierce kiss. I looked up at him with a worried expression.

"No, no, don't look like that. I'm okay, I'm under control. It's just that I'm impatient for all these arrangements to come to an end."

I told Max our waiting was worth it.

Chapter 20

❦

HOW DO WE LIVE?

With three of us in our duplexes working for good solutions to our living arrangements, it continued to sort itself out. The boys went back to school, found girlfriends, and brought them home one weekend to meet us. The girls were friendly, and fascinated by how I did things. I told them I just did them slower, and used a rolling cart to deliver items to rooms. Then it didn't seem to phase anyone that the boys had a handicapped mother. It was soon overlooked.

Another year sped by with a new book in print, a glorious garden overflowing with vegetables and flowers, and the office practice gaining great ground. I was delighted with the news one weekend when the boys were home, that they had become engaged, and had plans to marry after graduation. Their years at Yale were coming to an end. Dean was graduating in architecture, and Alan in engineering. Only seven months for my contract to expire.

. . .

How quickly things change. Till death do we part, I thought, as I looked out the kitchen windows, remembering the devastating scene at the edge of the vegetable garden. I had called 911 for an ambulance, gathered my crutches, and moved as fast as I was able to get to him where he had fallen.

I felt for a pulse, but he was gone. He was reposing in a place he loved. The silent smile on his face gave testimony to something I didn't know. I cried sorrowful and bitter tears.

When the EMTs arrived, resuscitation was applied, but he couldn't be revived. The birds continued to sing, and the world hadn't come to a stop, yet this man had passed into another dimension and there was no outward sign of it.

Julian was lifted to a gurney and covered with a blue striped blanket. They crossed the lawn, and he was placed in the ambulance. Quiet words were spoken to me, as I answered questions. As the ambulance backed out of the driveway, I realized this was Julian's last trip away from his home with Paul. Then I remembered Paul. Although he was in New York attending a meeting, I had a number where he could be reached.

I slowly entered the house, placed the call to New York, and knew how totally undone this would make him. I mentally prepared myself for the final confrontation. Another thought invaded as I waited for an aide to get Paul from his meeting.

As I had stood outside near Julian's body saying a silent prayer and thanking Julian for the intelligence, love, and insights he had given me, I realized I was no longer tied to this living arrangement. His death had become the knife that would cut through the connecting walls of the duplex, and quite literally release me for the first time in all those trying years. The aide came on the line to say Paul would call back in a few minutes.

I'm always making tea in a crisis, I told myself as I poured water into the tea kettle. I smiled a sad smile as I took down the tea box. Julian had brought the tea over a week ago, along with some bakery cookies.

I waited for Paul to call, sipping my tea and celebrating Julian's life. At least I could do that. The telephone jangled bringing me to the present and my next task.

"What is the emergency? I'm in an important meeting." Paul said his voice full of urgency.

"I called you right away. There has been a tragedy here. I won't soften it for you. It's Julian. He was working in the garden most of the morning and had a fatal heart attack about a half hour ago."

I heard Paul gasp out, "Oh, no."

"I called the EMTs, and they did all they could, but he was gone. He is at the Grover Hospital. You can call there and make arrangements. I have the number."

"Oh God, no! I could have stayed home, instead of coming here. Was he in any pain, did he suffer before we lost him?"

His questions begged me to assure him that Julian had died comfortably. I heard the tears and anguish in his voice.

"I will tell you some special last things he told me before he went into the garden, but not over the phone. When you get here there will be a lot of things to discuss."

"I'll catch an early flight back," he said with a sob, absorbed in his own misery, and I gave him the hospital number.

I went back to my tea to find it cold, and put the pretty white kettle on the burner for reheating. Julian had found the tea pot for me in Stockholm, on one of his trips. The pot was ringed with children in bright costumes of all nations.

That remembrance brought me to Max, and all the children he had helped.

No, let's not think of Max now. Save that for later in private when all this is behind me. Think of Julian, there are things to tell Paul.

It was noon as Julian stood in the doorway of my kitchen, wearing gardening gear, shaking seed packets invitingly.

"I'm growing some more delphiniums and nasturtiums for you this summer, and I think I have the solution to the tomato problem."

"Oh do you?" I asked, "Not like those pathetic ones we had last year?"

He laughed. "I bought some hardy plants that are three feet tall and loaded with yellow blossoms. I'll have a great crop.

"What's the news on the book?" He asked. "What's completed?"

"About fourteen chapters, it's sort of autobiographical. It's about our lives," I told him with honesty.

"Good," he nodded. "I know you will do it well. Your generosity has given me back my life. I've never been happier. There is no other woman who would have been so fair and understanding with Paul."

Yes, Julian, we are the only two who know that.

Paul had said 'we' in reference to his loss of Julian. How like him to lump us together, joined in a single relationship. But I hadn't thought that way before, I had only lived that way. I had had their love, the unusual love of two men, who loved each other. Now it was over.

A part of my brain jumped to what I would do next. Where do I go, how do I make the first move? Okay, they had needed my control and ideas before. They'll be needed again. It was time to call the children, tell them what's happened, and get some feedback on what they think.

As I rose from my chair, I was again accosted with the phrase, 'Till death do we really part.'

Paul wasn't going to like this one bit.

. . .

How brave is the world of lovers, I thought, sitting beside Paul at Julian's funeral. Selfishly they shared their precious and private moments shutting out others. They stretched forward, defying time, place, and intrusion. They emerged whole from the magical thrall to blink in wonderment at reality.

But I didn't emerge whole. I pieced myself together the best I could, and moved about with breezes of vulnerability blowing through the holes. A trust had been broken. Its damaging poison had seeped into my judgment at times, and the opportunity for lasting amends was forever lost. But, then, Paul wanted it that way.

Paul's character was shallow in that regard. I hadn't known, for he had been so wonderful in the beginning. He had anticipated all my early needs. But he had a 'hero's complex, ' and played it to the hilt. I may have forgiven him, but I would never forget.

During all this time I had never stepped over the final line in moral behavior. For me, it was unthinkable. I looked at the pure white flowers that blanketed Julian's casket. Purety not always of thought. Somewhere in my subconscious I had rationalized I was living a plan and had to see it through, and it wasn't just being virtuous.

Did my actions preserve the peace? Did our futures turn out better? I would like to think they did. It's a terrible ache to have an all-consuming love for someone and not be able to express it, so I knew how they had felt. Sometimes it carried me through down-times, just knowing it was love we were all grappling with. At first I drew on its promise and then saw it slowly fade away from me like the illusion it was. Oh, I know they loved me in their way, but it just wasn't enough. The 'what might have beens' are the cruelest teasers of our life.

How did my self-image fit in the picture? Is it more important earning the regard of others, doing the sacrificing, or doing just what you want? How about carefully investing your assets, or elevating your lifestyle to match others? Or expanding your horizons, or helping someone else reach theirs?

God, all this thinking! It was time for me to go to Maine. Julian would have understood. But first I had a more pleasurable engagement to fulfill.

A week later I celebrated my forty-fifth birthday in Boston with Dean and Alan and their wives. I had also invited my agent, editor, and two friends. I sat eating eggplant parmesan, drinking a cool glass of chianti, and looking around at the nine of us as we ringed the table. While I savored my delicious meal, I thought over my needed vacation. As the others chatted over their meals, I decided just where I was going.

I will drive up the East Coast to Camden, Maine. Driving time, five hours. I will stay at the Black Horse Inn nestled below the Camden Hills for two days of rest. Then I will proceed on to Bar Harbor for a week of looking around. There I can stay in town at the Windjammers Inn. It's walking distance to the harbor.

I will browse the shops, buy real gem jewelry, enjoy hot clam chowder while watching the beautiful yachts ply the waters. I will purchase creamy fudge in chocolate-walnut, and a hooded sweatshirt that has an embroidered sailboat on the front.

On a perfect day I will drive the coast road, take a picnic up to the top of Cadillac Mountain, and watch the sunset. I'll come down the switchback roads to the twinkling lights of Bar Harbor and have a lobster dinner.

My perspective will change with the height and breath of sea air and vista, and I will think, plan, and start a new book. Perhaps I will use that setting. Who knows? All that without a man, a husband, or a lover, because that part of my life has been swept away.

What a wonderful dream, but I knew I would no doubt end up at the Boothbay house instead. More practical, and I could get some needed chores finished.

I must have had a glazed look on my face, for Dean nudged me back to reality. "Mom, are you with us? You looked a million miles away." He leaned back from the table watching me with the blue of his father's eyes.

"Not quite a million," I corrected patting his hand, "But somewhere very romantic and delightful. I need a little time away now to start thinking about a new book, one I already have buzzing around in my head."

I knew he would approve.

Alan got my attention by clearing his throat, "I can accept your decision to live in the Maine house, but you know you need help occasionally. Can you get someone to come in and take over the chores?"

"My dear," I said smiling at his concern, "I've already seen to that. All of you here at this table are a central part of my life, and I'll only be a telephone or e-mail away."

Dean took up a new thought, "But you've been the catalyst all our lives, we've leaned on you, and we still need your input."

"You'll still get it whenever you want, I'll be there to listen and give support, just as you do for me. Now I want to hear how your projects are going at the office, fill me in one the details."

. . .

On the way back to my hotel in the cab, Marcia asked, "I noticed a change back there at the restaurant, you were almost melancholy. Was it your birthday, the candles and wine, or something else?"

"Yes, you're absolutely right. I was getting maudlin, and that's not healthy. I don't allow my characters in the books to do that, and I don't need it. I had been wondering about where I was going from here, and I decided I was going to go to Maine."

What had Max said about moods, ones that were sad? 'Mentally reduce them to stamps, paste them to envelopes, and send them away.'

I like that, but sometimes it takes a lot of persuasion to get my mind to concur.

Chapter 21

❦

COMMON GROUND

A cold wind had swept down from the Maritimes in the night, and although early summer had arrived, the house creaked with the cold. I burrowed deeper into my blankets resenting that I had to get up, it was daylight and the birds were singing. The furnace kicked on and shuddered through the ducts, and still I resisted facing the day.

I was here for shelter. Shelter from emotional storms. This had always been my haven, a place to sort, heal, and get inspiration from the view. The one across the waters to the Thread of Life. Now it was legally mine.

When I had driven up, I reveled in the distances, the light traffic, and the bright greens of the trees. I had stopped in a small market to get a bag of supplies, and purchased a bouquet of brave yellow tulips. I had looked forward to a cup of hot cocoa near the windows overlooking the ocean, and being in my sanctuary.

When I had entered the house, I had called out as I always did, "Hello House," and felt the ghosts of past experiences sweep out the door.

Funny how that worked.

Stretching now, I somehow made it from the bed and into the kitchen. Out in the bay a southwesterly whipped the water into white caps, and the sun sent rays spilling out to brighten the day. Here I was alone, my boys concerned, and Paul, well, Paul. I was also free, released, and settled. Ready to start a new life, but not sure if I were ready.

Remembering one of the last details in sorting out our lives, I mentally went over how smoothly it had all ended.

· · ·

Paul, Alan, Dean and I had been sittings around the kitchen table of my duplex. Each of us had a tablet and pen to take notes. A plate of double-fudge brownies tempted in the middle of the table. Dean sat munching a brownie watching his father. Alan broke his brownie into little pieces staring at his plate. They were all waiting for me to begin how the households were to be divided and what the living arrangements would be.

This was the first time Paul would be living on his own. He had gone from his parent's home into marriage, and then to live with Julian. Paul had decided to stay in his duplex, rent my side out, and take care of Julian's garden.

"Okay guys," I said, "this is what I've worked out." All eyes turned my way.

"Alan, you and Dean pick out furniture you want for your places, and mark them with colored tags. I'm only taking linens and my clothes. Paul, you can move all the foods and canned goods to your side, and that should solve that detail."

Paul's eyes flickered for a moment as though he had been caught in a sudden memory, and was now slowly returning to the conversation. He looked at me now understanding I was leaving for Maine, and he didn't quite want to let go of his need to control my life. The boys however, were more accepting of the plans.

We accomplished a great deal that day without a problem, and it was the last time we did so as a family.

. . .

As the Maine breezes swept over the water, I stirred my hot cocoa, nibbled toast, and asked the kitchen, What do I want in my life now? I have security, a career, and I own this house. I even have good investments. What's next? No need to go over sad endings. But am I ready to take on this new independence?

Straightening my shoulders and getting to my feet, I decided to start on a project that had been facing me for some time. In the bedroom were five packing cartons from a moving company. They were waiting for Paul's belongings. I attacked the job with vigor keeping a tally as I packed, and felt a catharsis as I marked and sealed box after box. It took most of the day to complete the chore, and by evening I was muscle-sore and dirty. A long soak in a hot bath lulled me into an early turn-in.

For several days I cleaned, sorted, ran a laundry, and put things into a new order.

On the fourth day, I was arranging games in the guest room closet where I keep extra blankets when the phone rang. As I passed the hallway mirror, I saw my reflection and grimaced. I look pretty mussed. I only hoped the call wasn't from Paul. I didn't want to hear from him.

When I answered the insistent ringing of the phone and heard the voice at the other end, I was instantly surprised. "Ooh, Max, how did you find me?"

"You know when you say, 'Oh Max,' it does things to me," he breathed in my ear, so far away on the line.

"Oh, Max."

"See, there you go again. What are you doing right now?"

"Let's see, cleaning house, or rather cleaning out the house. Why?"

"I'd like to take you to lunch."

"Where are you, you rascal?" I was incredulous, pleased and excited.

"About two miles down the road," he laughed. "I've been driving forever, and I'm hungry. I'm calling from a market. Do you need anything while I'm here?"

"No, just you. Come quickly. I have plenty for lunch. I can't wait to see you."

I was turning in half circles, this way and that, winding the telephone cord around my waist.

"And I you, dear heart. Put out some wine glasses. We have things to celebrate."

As we rang off, I rushed to clean up. No time for a shower, but I washed my face and hands, brushed my hair, and pulled it back with two combs. My hands were shaking as I applied a swipe of lipstick. I felt like I was going to burst with anticipation.

Already his car was coming down the lane crunching on the gravel driveway, and I went to meet him.

He moved from the driver's side, looked up and saw me open the screen door.

"Hi, let me get my valise first," he called out. "I'll be there in a minute."

He looked happy, full of energy, and excited to be here. He took from the passenger side a wicker basket and an overnight bag, and bounded up the steps.

"So this is your hideaway. Nice. You look wonderful!"

When Max crossed the deck, I couldn't get enough of his look. He was full of anticipation and joy, his face suffused with it. I felt myself shiver as my emotions started to spill over. He watched me reading what was going on with me.

He placed his valise and basket down on the deck, reached for me, crushed me to his chest, and all the years of longing and waiting shook loose. They became the tears that cascaded down my cheeks and onto his soft jacket. My sobs began and welled up to shake us both and I couldn't seem to control them.

"What's this? Don't get me started too," he said, his voice scratchy with emotion.

He held me tighter rubbing my back with small pats, crooning to me in soothing murmurs.

"I know. I know, love. You've had so many decisions to make, and all alone. Well, you're not alone now, and I intend to make up for lost time. We'll hash this all out later. So let me dry those tears and we'll go inside and you can show me your hideaway."

He produced a spotless handkerchief and dabbed at my cheeks making me smile at my foolishness. I in turn took the cloth from his hand and wiped off his jacket. His expression almost took my breath away. It was desire and a whole lot more, and he knew I felt it.

Finally he asked, "Now where is the kitchen? I need to drop off this food basket, and then my case in the guestroom.

I plan to be here for a while. Didn't know you were going to have a guest, did you?"

"How did you know I was here?" I asked as I moved through the doorway.

"Ah, my secret source. Your very helpful mother. God, bless her. She almost sent me here, not that I needed a push."

Going into the house in front of him, I couldn't think straight, but he headed for the kitchen to place the basket on the table. He then returned to the hallway for the tour. I led him down toward the bedrooms touching the wall here and there for balance.

Going down the hall we passed the master bedroom and Max noticed the boxes going to Paul.

"I'm really glad to see those," he said with conviction, a note of anger in his voice.

"They are going out tomorrow at eight by moving van," I assured him.

He turned suddenly to me, holding out his arms. "Come here."

I went to him, and he cradled me in his arms. "Could we have lunch, open the wine? I feel like tying one on."

Fun crackled in the air, and I replied laughing, "It's okay with me, the sky's the limit. I'll warm the soup and then we will see what happens."

"Yes, we'll see what happens," he said with hidden meaning in his eyes.

"May I build a fire in your fireplace?" he asked.

"Sure thing," I told him, "We can then eat at the coffee table."

I regrettably extricated myself from his arms. In the guest bedroom, Max took off his jacket, folded it and placed it on the bed. He rubbed his hands together looked at me and asked, "I think that bathroom is for me over there. Mind if I freshen up before we have our wine?"

I nodded in a daze and carefully made my way back to the

kitchen. I opened the hamper and found gourmet goodies, some canned, bottled, boxed and packaged. I was holding a can of mixed nuts aloft reading the label when I felt Max's presence.

He was standing in the doorway, his hands pressing the door jamb on either side looking washed and amused. He dropped his hands and came to stand behind me, using those hands to hold my waist. I forgot what I was reading.

I leaned back into him and he kissed my hair.

"In case you don't know, I'm here for the time it takes for you to know and understand how I feel, and for me to get answers. Those I want from you.

"So, in changing the subject, there are things in that basket that I like, such as caviar and cracked pepper biscuits, sausage, and salsa. You I know will prefer the nuts, marzipan, Gouda cheese, and lemon bread."

"I noticed you brought Granny Smith apples too," I said in a tiny voice, for I still couldn't quite speak in a normal tone.

"All this will go well with the vegetable soup I made this morning," I said, my voice now quivering, "but I don't know if I want to go and heat it, because I can't bear to move."

Max slowly turned me around to face him, gripped my shoulders and then raised his hands to cup my face. He brought his mouth to mine in an aching kiss that sealed my fate, as if it hadn't been decided a long time ago. Knowing how I felt, he chuckled, and that sent a deep rumble to his chest.

I was ready for more kisses, but he didn't seem to want to overwhelm me, and suggested lunch was now on the agenda. He moved away and I felt the parting like a cold wind.

It was all I could do to go through the motions of putting together a meal; I was rattled, thrilled, unsteady, my heart beating in overtime. He too seemed a little rocky as he made his way to the living-room to light a fire in the fireplace.

Steadying my breath, and concentrating on the chore at hand, I soon had our lunch tray set with soup bowls and silverware. What is Max doing? I sliced apples and cheese, unwrapped cookies, and placed them on plates.

The soup was ready when Max came into the kitchen to help carry the tray. We kept giving each other expectant looks like it was imperative we make contact. The air between us was charged and we loved it—drawing the agony out.

Max picked up our laden tray and started for the living-room.

I directed my next inquiry to his retreating back, "Are you going to make love to me?"

Max stopped short and slowly turned around with the most expectant and amused look on his face.

"What made you say that?" he asked in awe, eyes twinkling.

I backed into the counter as he came forward to set the tray on the table. He came closer and placed one hand on either side of me gripping the counter edge.

My head was down as I looked at the floor trying to explain, "I'm sorry I blurted that out. It just seemed that we were always saying hello and goodbye, always skirting our real feelings in a guarded way. The flashbacks suddenly converged, and I couldn't stand it."

Max studied me as I lifted my eyes to his. He nodded his head at my words.

"Don't be sorry you brought the subject out in the open, you're entitled. And the answer to your question is yes, after you're used to me."

I placed my hand on his chest, "I'm used to you, comfortable with you, and I've never trusted any man as much as you," my voice finally steady and full of conviction.

"That's quite a declaration, and it makes my approach easier. I don't want mindless sex with you, I want something patient and loving, and I know you do too. Let's enjoy our discovery of each other now in this different environment, this climate of freedom; let us savor these moments. You're a romantic, and I intend to not forget it. Are we in agreement?"

"Yes, I love that about you. You make things clear about where we both stand. I was beginning to feel out of control."

I remained by the counter taking easy breaths as Max moved back to pick up the food tray.

He spoke again giving me a rueful smile.

"You really had me there for a moment. I've never before been asked that question. I almost dropped the tray."

I had to laugh at the predicament in which I had placed him, but as usual he had handled it with gentleness and tact.

Max carried the tray to the coffee table and came back to open the wine. He poured the citron colored liquid into flutes and tasted a sip.

"This is superb. Apt for what I want to do."

He offered his glass to me, and I tasted it while looking into his eyes. Those blues penetrated. He leaned in to kiss me, and took the drink from my hand. The wine tasted even better from his lips

"One glass, one love for all time. We share from now on, Francy, as lovers do when they are just discovering what it is all about."

My eyes shimmered with renewed tears caused by his lovely words.

Clearing my throat from newly cast emotion, I said, "Will you teach me what it is all about, Max?"

I received a riveting look as he answered, "Most assuredly."

He belongs here.

Max stepped to the window then, his attention caught by the sound of a lobster boat going by. "Let me show you what you're seeing out there besides lobster boats," I said, moving into the warmth of his right arm.

"There was a time in the 1960 and 1970's when shrimp was the main industry here. Then the shrimp disappeared, and lobstering took over, with a few draggers working out of the area for cod and haddock.

"Many boats come to Boothbay Harbor each summer, making it probably as crowded as a hundred years ago. When we get unsettled weather and it drives in a big blow, as many as four hundred mackerel schooners, coasting vessels, and banks schooners come for shelter. I've driven down to Ocean Point to see them come in.

"Now, if you want to sail these waters coming east out of Boothbay past Ocean Point, you have three alternatives. The tide may dictate your choice. The ebb out of the Damariscotta River can be formidable, so you may not want to ford that stream.

"Then, Christmas Cove to starboard, where you are now looking, offers a harbor and several nice places to eat. It's also easy to sail in and out of the harbor once you escape the grip of the current in the main river. The third way is to tack to the starboard past Christmas Cove directly into the Thread of Life passage. From there you will find John's Bay, an immense watercourse ending in the east by Pemiquid Lighthouse. It's a beautiful trip."

"Very informative," he agreed, "and yes, I'd like to sail here. With you. But what did you say about a thread of life? Somehow that strikes me as something familiar."

Max looked perplexed for a moment.

"Oh yes, the Thread of Life," I answered. "It was named by a minister in the1800's. It comes from scripture. Now, let's go enjoy the fire you made."

I moved carefully, edging toward the sofa as Max set the tray on the coffee table.

In front of the fire that looked as good as it smelled, we started on the wine. Max sat in an armchair near the couch. There was so much tension spanning the distance between us, I could almost reach out and touch it. I glided over the idea that we might not eat lunch after all.

Don't hurry, slow down I warned myself.

Max seemed composed though, but then he always did. I wanted to watch what he said and how he said it. He was starting to romance me, and I loved it. I felt young, adored, and safe. At my age and his we were testing some old truths, and I knew he felt sure where he was headed.

Max took a bite of a cracker and chewed in thought. He stretched out his legs, crossing his ankles, totally relaxed. Obviously he had a lot on his mind. The burning logs snapped a counterpoint to the sparks in the air.

"Francy, you've recently ended something, and I'm now about to start something. Are you with me?"

"Yes," my voice came out with a strange quiver.

"Your mother hit the high spots of the last six months," he began, "and I'd like your take on where you are now in your thinking. You will wrestle with memories and questions for a while, and I'll be here to listen and put your doubts to rest if I can."

"I need your input always," I confessed, "as I did in the past." But, now I haven't anything to unload. I had two years to come to grips with who I was and where I was going. Lately, I just had questions from family and friends to appease.

"You, to me, are a breath of fresh air, more familiar and beloved. I can look at you with love and desire, flirt with you, and have a new beginning. Understand, my heart is not burdened, and I'm no man's wife."

Max leaned toward me expectantly, pain a quick spasm across his face quickly wiped away by a look of yearning.

I took his hand in mine, "I'm fine, squarely on my own two feet."

Max shook his head in wonder, "And I wish to sweep you off them. I'm caught between wanting to leap and standing still, giving you time and eclipsing it. But I know you have more to tell me, so I'll settle down for now."

"No," I said, "only one small detail, then I am finished. Paul and I handled all the last details with a minimum of emotion whenever we were together, and usually one of the boys or both were with us. Paul did kiss me goodbye just before I drove away from the duplex, just like he still had the right."

My expression was hard as I told the particulars revealing how I had felt at the time.

"No more loose ends? No tangibles or intangibles to iron out?" Max asked seriously.

I shook my head, sighed heavily, and leveled my eyes with his.

Max nodded at me, thinking, but deciding to not carry the subject any further. He was satisfied with the answers I had given him.

"Time for more truths on my side. I had snippets of suspicion about Paul and how you were being treated. I vacillated between anger and frustration during this past year. I wanted to wrench you out of that house, but was powerless to carry it through. So I stood by and kept myself busy.

"I had a trip to take to Nairobi for the World Health Organization. Once there, I visited a new hospital, and was directed to the room of a young man around nineteen or twenty years of age. He was paralyzed in both legs and one arm from Polio, and was angry and uncooperative.

"I found myself sitting by his bed telling him about you. Your struggles caught his attention, and he started asking questions. He eventually became amused with the story about your list of ten things you hated most.

"Later I learned he adopted your approach, fitted it to his own problems, and began to solve them one by one."

I shut my eyes imagining the scene, and clasped both hands over my heart savoring the essence of the story. How dear, how precious that Max had used my experience to open the mind of one stricken. Only Max would be that sensitive to the boy's needs as he had been to mine.

"On another note, and we're changing the subject again, I haven't lost any of my feelings for you. I can now legally pursue my intentions."

"And, what are your intentions?" I asked breathlessly.

"In the short term, nothing really honorable. But in the long one, something entirely wholesome."

He studied my reaction, pursing his lips, noting my flushed face.

"You're scared, aren't you? Are you afraid of me, or going forward with your own feelings?"

"Both," I said fretfully.

He chuckled at my answer and poured more wine in my glass.

"This will help the jitters, quiet the stomach, and erase the turmoil. It will be salubrious, you of the big words. Leave it all behind, Francy. You're in my hands now, I won't let you down."

"You know, Max, I learned a lot over the years, and a lot from Paul. He learned from me also. It wasn't all for naught."

I must have looked like I was pleading for his understanding.

"Writers, 'for naught, ' I love that. But you are generous. I would never have defended him. Although I see your point. My biggest problem was I wanted to be in his shoes. I wanted his wife. I still do. Plain and simple."

I took a deep breath, delight spreading like an advancing wave. "Can you guess what I have always loved about you? What makes me melt?"

His eyes glittered with humor. He shook his head.

"Your wrist with your watch on it, and the way your hair in back just touches the collar of your shirt, and especially the way you explain things to me."

His eyes lit up. "Oh you're observant all right. I'll keep that in mind. You know what gets to me?"

I shook my head, feeling suddenly shy.

"The way you look at me following each word. I sometimes forget what I'm saying. Your humor is wonderful, and you have a way of tilting your head to one side as you consider something. You talk about melting, I have visions I couldn't describe. I'd rather show you. Besides you're using delaying tactics, and they won't work any more."

I held a breath as color again suffused my entire body. He

had set off sparks I had no intention of extinguishing. It wasn't just glimmer and sparkle, it was flash. It shot out in all directions, eclipsing all the past events.

Oh, how pleased he seemed to be with himself as he came to the couch and rolled me into his arms. Does the meltdown begin now?

Chapter 22

❦

ULTIMATE ECSTASY

We decided the next day, after the movers collected the boxes, to drive to Bar Harbor and continue this romantic and impromptu vacation. Max made reservations for us at the Outsiders Inn.

On the drive up the coast, we stopped in little coves to look around and take pictures. One cove was so full of lobster markers we could almost walk across them to a distant island. Fishing shacks, some remodeled and others precariously perched, dotted the shoreline. Easy flowing water lapped at pilings that supported long, sun-bleached wharfs, while snowy sea gulls eyed everything that moved. The salt air was light, and banked clouds moved slowly to the north.

What a beautiful day, holding such expectations. It was almost as though I'd never been there before, but then I had never seen these places with Max; they seemed to take on a different hue. We were also very aware of each other, touching, smiling into each other's faces like imps.

Moving on, we eventually drove over the causeway and into Bar Harbor. There we checked in to our lodgings and proceeded to browse the stores. We walked into the Acadia Fudge Shop on Main street picking up aromas of chocolate and vanilla that permeated the walls. It was a clean, neat store that had glass cases filled with blocks of fudge pilled into pyramids. Several people were being waited on by the saleslady, and we moved up to wait behind them.

Our day had been spent discovering things together. We had deliberated over paintings and model ships, buying all sorts of surprise items and filling the trunk of Max's car with bulging paper bags. This shop only added to our tastes. But before long we found we were arguing over which type of fudge to buy.

I turned to ask, "Max, what flavor do you really want?"

Instead of answering he drew me into his arms before I could react. Then I began to struggle, feeling the embarrassment of eyes on us. He held me tighter.

"I know exactly what I want, and it's you. Will you marry me?" he asked, face flushed with excitement.

An expectant hush fell over the other customers in the store as they awaited my answer. I gaped at Max, realizing he was serious, for he didn't let go.

"Yes, yes, yes," I breathed before I was soundly kissed. Applause all around greeted us as we parted. I also heard a few sighs that weren't my own.

"Now, I wish to purchase two pounds of the chocolate mint," Max announced to the saleslady, pointing to the stack of pale green and chocolate, "and a pound of vanilla-walnut for my bride-to-be."

The saleslady beamed a broad smile, reached across the counter, and took hold of his hand saying, "Congratulations, and I'll throw in a half-pound of chocolate-macadamia as a gift."

Back in the car, we each devoured two pieces of fudge to celebrate, then drove to the Acadia park opening that would take us up the switchbacks to the top of Cadillac Mountain. We reached the summit just as the setting sun bathed the clouds and granite rocks a glorious pink, and clear, cool night crept in.

Such a vista! We could look in all directions and take in scenes of wonder. Toy cities dotted the far horizon and mountains in dark shapes rose in way-off New Hampshire. We got out of the car, walked to the parapet, and looked down on the twinkling lights of Bar Harbor. Out in Frenchmen's bay two large sailboats tacked back and forth, and to the east a moon sliver glowed orange above ocean mists.

I shivered in the cool night air. Max remarked, "I'll have to smother you in furs to keep you warm. I like the idea."

Laughing at the mental picture, I said, "Furred to the Max?"

"Now you're talking," he said, admiring my play on words.

As we stood taking in the marvels of our view, Max put his arm around me and pulled me close. Just then, on a high outcropping a bagpiper began the lilting tones of a Scottish song. We felt surrounded by enchantment.

Max hadn't arranged this, but I know who had.

Max couldn't think of a better accompaniment to our visit on such a day. A day that gave us a future together. As the music drifted over the scrubby pine, Max kissed me with passion, and I returned his kiss, lost in the magic of where we were and the promises of tomorrow.

When we parted, Max said, "Despite all this vastness, I don't feel insignificant at all. I've just this day won the heart of my love."

I squeezed his arm. "No Max, not just today. You've always had a claim. Right back to the time you peeled that apple for me. It was almost like Adam and Eve, but in reverse order."

Max chuckled in wonder. "So, that's when we first tempted fate? Somehow in life we managed to sidestep the snake."

I tossed my head back, smiling. "When you broke your leg, and I came to see you, the snake almost got the better of me."

Once returning to the harbor, Max parked on a downtown side street, and we walked to the Jolly Roger for dinner. We had a table near the windows, and could look out over the wharf and see the two lovely windjammers, now all lit up with twinkle lights tacking back and forth in the harbor.

Max ordered lobster for both of us, and spent some time reading the wine menu until he made his selection. Always a man for careful details. Perhaps that was one more reason I loved him.

An hour later, Max leaned back from the table, wiped his mouth with the linen napkin, and patted his middle in satisfaction. "A glass of excellent wine, a crust of bread, and thou. How could any man ask for more?"

His eyes sparkled as they met mine, and I lifted my glass in salute.

"Falling in love all over again is as heady as this wine," I said, "and my mind wars between extreme wonder and caution. When we are together, I'm breathless, my heart flip-flops, and I have this feeling of expectation all the time. However, on the cautious side, I wonder how our children will take our news?"

"They're adults, they have a life, and they understand love. How could they not be happy for us?" Max asked with assurance.

"Are there no barriers you can see?" I asked, hoping there was none.

"Nope, and I won't allow any. What I'm thinking is we will have plenty of time to sort things out." He massaged my hand with his in a lazy pattern.

"Know one thing," he said half in jest."I'm not marrying you for your money." We both laughed at that remark.

"I'd like us to live in my house, vacation in yours, and take trips to see the world. I plan to satisfy all your whims, dear heart, and I can't wait to get started. Are you ready, can you make the decision I've waited all these years to hear? But more importantly, is your 'Yes' unconditional?"

"No conditions, no barriers, no waiting. I'm all yours, to have and to hold, with all my love."

"Now you have me breathless and full of expectations." His facial expression told me he expected to fulfill all of them.

"Max, my love, you have my head spinning. Take this slowly, let me have time to get used to you," I pleaded, knowing the pace was picking up.

We strolled back to the car and once inside Max said, "I want to give you the moon."

"I've always wanted a piece of it," I said, lightening the moment.

"Don't level my remark, I'm serious." His voice low and intent.

"I know, my dear, I'm just a little excited. I want every second to last, to stretch out."

Oddly he seemed more relaxed than I, like he had made up his mind and was confident he was saying and doing all the right things. I only wished I felt the same way.

Max, in the dim light of the car, looked into my eyes. "I have a lot to discuss with you, all sorts of details. But first, a question, this is still burning. I've never heard you say it. Do you really love me?"

I was caught off-guard by the question. I put my hand over my heart, delaying my reply. He waited patiently.

I gave a heartfelt sigh, "Yes, so very much, my dearest love. Yes, I love you, deeply and deliriously."

Max wasted no time gathering me to him in an embrace. Then an inch from my lips said, "Such longing, the ache. I once thought I'd die with it."

My next words were lost in tears, and he smoothed them away. My memory flashed back to our time in the hospital when he brushed away my tears. Such a destiny, now sweet destiny.

"Where from here, Francy?" he ground out expectantly.

My voice breaking, "I want you to make love to me, and I want to be kissed until I'm delirious."

"My exact wish. How many times shall I kiss you?" he asked, getting into the play of it.

I replied happily, "Oh I don't know, maybe one hundred and one. That's always been a great number for us."

We drove to our inn, lazily walked the corridor, and Max slipped the key card into the slot to open the door. Soft music played in the suite, low lights warmed the rooms. In the bedroom, the king-sized bed covers had been turned down, my nightgown and his pajamas had been laid out. Wrapped chocolates rested on the pillows, and pink roses nodded casually from a large vase on the dresser.

Such sweetness came from the background music as I gathered my crutches next to me, looking about the rooms trying to decide what next to do. I hadn't noticed that the music was from *The Phantom of the Opera*.

Max came close to help me and I hoped he didn't notice I was shaking. If he did, he didn't let on.

Now is not the time for words to fail me, but they did. We had been heading for this moment for so long I couldn't believe it had arrived. It had everything, it enveloped us with rapture. Reaching for each other at the same moment, we knew we had so much to explore. We would that night give to each other the finest fiber of our beings.

I wasn't aware when Max turned off the music, for I had found ecstasy. The night deepened, the heavens hovered close, and the completion of our destinies became united in the stars.

That which is believed is love

EPILOGUE

Whenever I recited this story in the past, it brought a variety of responses. Sometimes there was understanding or wonder, but mostly it brought tears to the eyes of my listener. So I assumed it was told well.

From the time I was nineteen to the age of forty-five, I never forgave myself for contracting polio. Then, somehow, I did. Finally I understood I didn't go out and purposefully 'catch' it; it had rather, found me.

I learned valuable life lessons along the way: not pouring energy into places where it shouldn't go, not letting others lean, and finding a balance between what I could accomplish and what I hoped to achieve. Then there was the finding of shortcuts that created inventing, and getting others to match their pace with mine. I would always be adapting and adopting.

My celestial committee, faith in God, and a belief that love conquers all continue to be my tools. The writing of this novel, my struggles in life, decisions, and plans are never accomplished alone, I call out my vanguard.

My wish for the future is that science will find means to reverse paralysis, paralysis caused by any source.

THE
THREAD OF LIFE CHAIN

The Thread of Life is located in mid coast Maine. It is made up of rocky shoals and tiny islands. It is a place so named for a legendary escape by a good mariner fleeing a bad one. (As a sailor, he could cut off his course a half mile, if played well, by going from Damariscotta River, making a turn to the left to the Thread of Life, threading his way down the narrowing passage, passing through the "Needle's Eye" east of Turnip Island with a half fathom sounding, and breaking out into John's Bay.)

Jeremiah 51:13, Revised Standard Bible reads: The thread of life may be cut, that is, shortened—only by the eye of the needle. "You who live by mighty water, rich in treasures, Your end is come, The Thread of your Life is cut."

Matthew 19:24 reads: It is easier for a camel to go through the eye of a needle than for a rich man to enter the Kingdom of God.

THINGS YOU MIGHT
WANT TO KNOW

Poliomyelitis, or infantile paralysis, is endemic in all parts of the world, but epidemics didn't appear until the latter part of the nineteenth century. A major outbreak occurred in Stockholm, Sweden in 1887, and then the United States began to experience sporadic episodes. The actual isolation of the polio virus was achieved in 1908 by two Viennese scientists, Landsteiner and Popper.

ACUTE ANTERIO POLIOMYELITIS—FIRST PHASE

Polio is an acute viral infection made up of three strains: Brunhilde—Type 1, Lansing—Type 2, and Leon—Type 3. These strains have remained stable, and no new strains of the virus have been detected to date. The virus is transmitted by way of the mouth, is implanted in the walls of the pharynx and the intestinal tract, and enters the central nervous system, or CNS, via the bloodstream. The incubation time for the infection is seven to ten days. The site of the tissue destruction begins in the spinal cord (anterior horn), an area of nerve cells controlling the muscles.

This first phase starts suddenly and builds to severe headache, fever, stiff neck and back, and deep muscle pain. This phase is called a "prodrome," meaning there is no feeling of getting gradually sick. An elevated temperature is also found as the infection progresses. The surgical procedure called a spinal tap (lumbar puncture) during a major illness is conducted. A thin needle is inserted into the lower back between the bones of the spine and into the spinal canal. A small amount of fluid is extracted. Microscopic investigation of this fluid shows when polio is present, by demonstrating an increased white cell count (largely lymphocytes) sometimes reaching a thousand per cubic centimeter of fluid. Slightly increased protein is also evident.

MAJOR IllNESS—SECOND PHASE
This phase begins with flaccid paralysis of various muscle groups, and loss of superficial and deep reflexes. The site of paralysis depends on the location of lesions in the spinal cord or medulla. Fluid and electrolyte balances are supplied via IV, analgesics given for headaches, and applications of moist hot packs applied to limbs for pain and spasm.

BULBAR FORM OF POLIO
Bulbar polio is highly fatal. In this type, the cranial nerve muscles are involved. The early signs are difficulty in swallowing, nasal regurgitation, and a nasal voice.

In the febrile stage of illness, only weak analgesics can be used for pain due to depressed respiration. Emphasis is on rest, without strain or exertion.

Relief of muscle spasm comes through application of moist hot packs four to five times a day, and sometimes throughout the night when needed.

Children and adults in iron lungs, have their oxygen levels and pressure rates individually adjusted. Patients get oxygen inhalation, postural drainage, and removal of secretions by way of suction apparatus. There is a vacuum device to allow patients to cough or sigh. If this procedure causes complications, a tracheotomy is performed.

If the patient regains breathing ability, a several-day weaning process is started via a chest (cuirass) respirator.

During the day the patient is taken out of the iron lung and placed in a bed, and the respirator, small and portable, is strapped over the chest. A face mask is placed over the nose and mouth to supply oxygen. The patient goes back to the iron lung for the night.

THE IRON LUNG

The iron lung (respirator), developed by Drinker-Collins, was used extensively during the polio epidemics of the 1940's and 1950's for patients with bulbar polio. The apparatus was greatly feared. (It was thought of as certain death, or as a coffin.) The iron lung is a large metal tank resting horizontally on a wheeled rack that encases the whole body except for the head which rests outside on a padded platform. The neck of the patient is gripped by a sponge gasket or collar, to maintain pressures inside the tank. Bellows below the tank are set to alternate normal and low pressures of air inside the tank. This helps the patient breathe. A patient can be kept in this machine for long periods.

A procedure called a tracheotomy, a surgical opening of the windpipe at the base of the throat, is sometimes done when the patient's throat muscles became paralyzed. A breathing tube is inserted into the windpipe, and the pressurized air is forced in and the carbon dioxide forced out. The patient is fed via a nose or stomach tube infused with warm, nourishing liquids.

National Foundation for Infantile Paralysis— March of Dimes

In 1938, Basil O'Connor, former law partner of Franklin D. Roosevelt, President of the United States, and himself a victim of polio, set up the foundation as a fund raiser to conquer polio. The foundation awarded grants and fellowships to deserving scientists and doctors in the pursuit of discovering viruses. The March of Dimes was the idea of comedian Eddie

Cantor, told to the president. Much of the money collected from door to door was used in the care of polio patients.

The first International Poliomyelitis Conference was held in 1948 in New York City. Dr. Hart E. Van Riper, medical director of the National Foundation for Infantile Paralysis, said: "We may be fighting not one disease, but a whole family of slightly related diseases. We do know already that there are several strains of infantile paralysis capable of producing clinical symptoms, but we do not know how closely related these virus strains are, or, indeed, if they are biologically related at all. We do not know whether special measures of prevention or treatment are necessary for each individual type. Until this problem is solved, there can be no certain prevention or cure."

Enders—Weller—Robbins

In 1954, three doctors of bacteriology, having cultivated the polio virus in tissue cultures, were awarded the Nobel Prize. Their findings made it possible to produce large amounts of virus suitable for vaccine production.

SISTER KENNY—SALK—SABIN

Three important names are associated with the outbreak of polio: Sister Elizabeth Kenny, Dr. Jonas Salk, Dr. Albert Sabin, the two icons of immunization. Sister Elizabeth Kenny, a nurse from Australia, was the pioneer in the treatment of polio patients. She introduced and taught two programs: active physical therapy that would stimulate and reeducate paralyzed muscles, and the repeated use of hot baths, or the application of steamed towels for pain. She came to the United States in 1940 to establish the Sister Elizabeth Kenny Institute in Minneapolis, Minnesota. Her methods were slowly adopted in other states, and then were used extensively. Once asked how polio was contracted, she replied: "Nobody knows whether you drink it, eat it, or if it bites you."

Dr. Salk, a microbiologist, developed the first inactivated vaccine to combat Polio. In a massive experimental field test in 1953 and 1954, millions of Americans were immunized. The program was so successful that cases of the disease in Western Europe and North America plummeted from 75,000 in 1955 to less than 1,000 in 1963. The excitement engendered by that drama prompted optimistic declarations that the disease would soon be eradicated from the planet.

Dr. Sabin, another microbiologist, cultivated an oral, live-virus vaccine, and after 1957 field tests, it became the most widely used polio vaccine. The vaccine contains all three strains of the virus.

WHO

The World Health Organization (WHO)is still using the polio vaccine to immunize people in undeveloped nations. Of all the viral diseases affecting children, only smallpox has been mostly eradicated, but in Zambia, Zaire, and Malawi, where children have not been vaccinated, the disease still appears. The WHO and the Children's Vaccine Initiative are under the auspices of the United Nations, and they are addressing this problem. It is hoped that polio will truly be eradicated by the year 2010.

Brazil had major outbreaks of polio in the 1970's and 1980's, and through the Pan American Health Organization, the NPCP (National Poliomyelitis Control Program) was set up to immunize all the children. The incidence of polio in Brazil then was the highest in the world. Dr. Sabin, greatly admired there, came to inaugurate the plan. From 1985 to 1994 all the children were inoculated against polio in all of the Americas. Since 1994 the Americas have been free of endemic polio.

POST POLIO SYNDROME (PPS)

In the 1980's, a cruel reminder of the disease began to appear. Long-term survivors of polio were again having symptoms of pain in muscles and/or joints, fatigue, and loss of muscle strength. After careful diagnosis, for some conditions mimic PPS, they had to begin a precisely paced program of therapy. This condition was first called post polio muscular atrophy, but now is known as post polio syndrome.

The weakness, fatigue, and atrophy were felt to be most likely caused by a progressive deterioration of motor neurons. The muscle and joint pain is likely caused by chronic musculoskeletal "wear and tear."

DISABILITY

Millions of people have some form of disability due to birth, disease, or accident. People with disability have been treated with fear, suspicion, disregard, and jealousy, and have had to overcome crushing prejudice. The injustice of such treatment dwells in the hearts of those lacking in either a generous heart or spirit, much to their loss.

Technological and medical advances have placed many persons who are disabled into schools, work places, and sports competitions. Laws have been passed that have removed restrictive barriers, allowing persons with disabilities access to almost every location. The Americans with Disabilities Act, passed in 1990, provided comprehensive civil rights protection.

This was the first time persons with disabilities were recognized, not as a minority, but as contributing people.

FEET ACCOMPLI

When small piggies went to the market
she tiptoed around in her Twos
both feet were cased in pink stockings
in or out of Mary Jane shoes

She skipped on those toes in her childhood
then skated on ice after school
or raced a Schwinn in the country
and swam in the lakes and the pool

Teen toes took to heels in a sling-pump
to be graceful on feet was her aim
nineteen was her age as a coed
to give art a fling was the game

Her world became filled with a romance
and her life was finally on track
she walked with another on campus
as darkened clouds built at her back

For Polio took the momentum
and crushed independence so fast
it left her reduced in all motion
both her legs in thick plaster casts

The challenge was real, it was certain
to crawl and to stand was the test
determined in grace to be normal
get back all her life was the quest

Three years they would work for some progress
yet her man stood by the ordeal
never stopping to reconsider
through transfers and braces of steel

Her toes planted firm and for balance
with crutches designed by her love
she took tiny steps into sunlight
and knew she'd been heard from above

Two feet now led down to an altar
in a church with flowers in white
the marriage and joy that came after
made the strides to the future bright

They traveled to Europe together
saw riches of landscape and art
and toured the same roads as the ancients
their shoes only inches apart

Now three children followed this union
and grew up in sneakers to be
adults with kiddies in strollers
completing the whole family tree

Once more piggies go to the market
in walkers, or sandals, or heels
her feet keeping time with life's rhythm
just tapping out pleasure she feels

REFERENCES

The Polio Virus and the Vaccine
J. L. Melnick
World Health
1989

Tetraplegia and Paraplegia, 3d ed.
I. Bromley
1985

Handbook of Physical Therapy 3d ed.
Robert Istack
1977

Patenting the Sun: Saga of Jonas Salk
Jane S. Smith
1990

Grolier Electronic Encyclopedia
1995

Merck Manual of Diagnosis and Therapy
Merck Sharp & Dohme Research Laboratories
1966–1992–1995

The Coming Plague
Laurie Garrett
Farrar Straus and Giroux—New York
1994

Islands of the Mid Maine Coast
Charles B. McLane
Tilbury House Publishers
1994

Harvard Medical School—Department of Physical & Rehabilitation
Post-Polio Syndrome: Past, Present & Future
Symposium 1997

Polio
Thomas M. Daniel and Frederick C. Robbins
University of Rochester Press
1997